THE DIRTY BOMBERS

THE DIRTY BOMBERS

ED TAYLOR

Matador
9 Priory Business Park,
Wistow Road, Kibworth Beauchamp,
Leicestershire. LE8 0RX
Tel: (+44) 116 279 2299
Fax: (+44) 116 279 2277
Email: books@troubador.co.uk
Web: www.troubador.co.uk/matador

ISBN 978 1783060 443

British Library Cataloguing in Publication Data.
A catalogue record for this book is available from the British Library.

Typeset by Troubador Publishing Ltd, Leicester, UK
Printed and bound in the UK by TJ International, Padstow, Cornwall

Matador is an imprint of Troubador Publishing Ltd

For my grandchildren.

Chapter 1 – The End of the Beginning

Rork panted hard as he struggled to gain altitude. His lungs burned with the effort he was making and he felt a trickle of blood seeping from the corner of his beak. He could hear the roar of the great machines below him and smell their hot filthy breath as it gushed past him. Gradually, he climbed the steep sides of the quarry away from the dreadful sights he had witnessed. His wings felt unbearably heavy, and it took every ounce of his remaining strength to fly over the near-vertical edge to land clumsily on the rough pasture of the Downs. He lay face down for a few moments, relishing the smell and texture of the grass beneath him. He spread his wings and tried to absorb energy from the sun while controlling his rasping breath. His whole body began to tremble violently.

It may have been for a few seconds, or even 10 minutes, that Rork closed his eyes, but he was suddenly alerted by his sixth sense. He cautiously opened one eye and saw the head of a rabbit poking out of a burrow just a few yards away. The rabbit eyed him curiously and for a few moments Rork just stared back. Suddenly the rabbit glanced upwards and instantly disappeared back into his burrow. Rork sensed danger and turned to see a large crow hovering above him. "You are a bit early, my friend," shouted Rork, "I'm not ready for you just yet!" He waved a wing angrily at the crow, which flew off to find easier pickings elsewhere.

"Come on you fool, try to get a grip." He looked down at his breast and could see the blood still pulsing from the wound. "Must get to see the Admiral before it's too late." He stood and flapped his wings, ready for take-off, but it was a feeble effort and it left him panting painfully. Rork suddenly realised that he didn't have the power to rise from the ground by his own efforts and he almost despaired. He grimaced as he recognised the irony of his situation. His first stuttering flights as a fledgling had been over these same Downs, encouraged and guided by the beautiful Vena. He choked as he remembered the terrible end she had just met and his desire to avenge her re-ignited his determination. What would Vena have said?

Use the terrain to your advantage. Remember to seek the help of thermals. ***Soar!***

Although it was the last thing he wanted to do, Rork turned to face the quarry once more. He took a deep breath and, with more of a lurch than a run, launched himself into space. He deliberately avoided looking down at the landfill site in case emotion sucked him back once more. He glided round towards the Downs and, using his energy as sparingly as possible, sought the thermals that would take him up their slopes. Luckily for him, it was still high summer and the temperature inside the quarry was high. With the help of a warm but fetid air current, and calling on all of his flying skills and physical resources, Rork struggled to the top of the Downs.

Normally Rork loved this moment, as the view of the ancient port unfolded below him, but today all he felt was relief that he had escaped the carnage behind him, and that he would be able to carry his awful news to the Admiral. He took one last look at the quarry. He could clearly see the huge machines still working over the landfill site as if nothing had happened. His frail body shuddered as he remembered the dreadful sights he had witnessed and he turned to concentrate on the task ahead.

Below him, Barlmouth looked the same as it ever had. Rork reflected that this might be the last time he saw the view that his ancestors had seen for all those centuries before him. The tiny colour-washed houses with their grey slate roofs stepped down the hills that surrounded the harbour, huddling together for mutual protection, just like they always had. The steep road leading to the little town was packed with cars taking more and more holidaymakers to seek its charms. Rork could hear the sounds of the traffic now and the hooting of frustrated motorists as they waited for a tourists' coach to manoeuvre into the car park. He watched the fishing boats entering and leaving the harbour, plying their trade as pleasure boats for the tourists, instead of catching fish as they were designed and built to do. He wheeled gently ever lower and his keen sense of smell detected that familiar aroma of Cornish pasties, fish and chips and ice cream. He could see his friends circling and dipping at the edges of the harbour as they searched for any scraps the humans may leave behind. Two of them were his young cousins, and he made a mental note to caution Jez for taking unnecessary risks by going too close to the humans.

The sandy cove formed by the edge of the cliffs on one side and the huge harbour wall on the other was packed with holidaymakers roasting in the summer sun and squealing with delight as they entered the still chilly water of the sea. A crowd had gathered at the end of the harbour wall to watch teenage boys as they bravely jumped off the wall to bomb into the somewhat murky water of the harbour itself. Rork feared the Admiral would not be in his usual place because of the throng, but then he spotted the grand old bird gazing imperiously down from the green light that marked the starboard side of the entrance to the little port.

Rork knew he had to maintain speed and achieved this by losing height rapidly as his side slipped towards the harbour. As a result, he came in too fast and landed clumsily on the harbour wall itself, accidentally knocking into a young girl in his desperation to feel solid ground beneath his feet. The girl screamed and dropped her candyfloss in alarm. Her mother turned and tried frantically to shoo Rork away, but another woman intervened because she could see that Rork was injured. The commotion attracted the attention of the Admiral, who swooped swiftly down to Rork, screeching at the top of his voice and flapping his wings ferociously. The people nearby got his message and moved to what they deemed to be a safe distance. The Admiral strutted up and down, fixing his one beady eye firmly on them, as if daring them to come closer.

Rork tried to speak. "Just take it easy, boy. Get your breath back," said the Admiral gruffly. Rork looked at him gratefully. No wonder this grand old bird was their leader. Although he was now physically showing his age, the Admiral still exuded wonderful presence. His feathers were scuffed and torn in places and there was a tear in his webbed feet. His empty eye socket glowed angrily red, but despite all this, and his great age, he still carried himself proudly erect. He was an immense bird and he must have been one hell of a scrapper in his youth, thought Rork.

"The Quarry" he croaked, "there's been a massacre! They're dead… all DEAD!"

"Dead? Who's dead?" said the Admiral, – more sharply this time.

"All of them, "cried Rork. "Slet and Vena… Jee and Dostin… – even some of the babies. It was awf-"

"What happened? What killed them? WHO killed them? Take your time and tell me from the beginning, Rork."

Rork recovered himself slowly. "We were there – all of us -spread over the new tippings just like we have done many times before. Vena called out to me that she had just found something very tasty, but as I flew over to join her, there was an enormous bang. When I looked again, she had disappeared in a cloud of feathers." Rork choked once more, filled with emotion. "One of her wings just floated down out of the air and landed beside me. It was perfect – as though she had never been touched," he sobbed. "But she had just disappeared." Rork paused, just unable to continue for the moment. "We all screamed in alarm and tried to fly away, but more dreadful bangs followed. We were just getting knocked out of the sky one by one. I could see humans at the end of the tip holding black rods and before the bangs came I could see the rods flash and make smoke. Whatever it was cut Dostin in two and made great holes in the others. I was hit in the chest and had the air knocked out of me. I fell to the ground and landed behind a piece of tin. I must have passed out for a few minutes and perhaps that is what saved me. The humans must have thought I was dead. When I awoke, they had gone – apart from the men in the big machines. They were driving over the ground where we had been feeding, pushing more rubbish over our dead bodies."

The concerned holidaymakers came closer. "We must do something for the poor thing, he looks so very frail." The Admiral flapped his wings and screeched ear-piercingly so that they quickly got the message and moved away again. "He is trying to protect him, when all we really want to do is help," said the mother of the child.

The Admiral looked back at Rork. "We must call a meeting of the Colony. This is so dreadfully serious that we must get everyone there. You can tell them the entire story then."

"I'm not sure I'll be able to make a meeting," said Rork weakly, "I think I'm dying, Sir."

"Nonsense," roared the Admiral. "Don't think like that. We're going to need brave young gulls like you if we are going to come through this together." Rork felt his chest puff with pride. The Admiral looked about him, as if searching for help.

"Do you think you can make it to Turan's cave?" he asked. "She will help you get fixed up. It looks like a flesh wound to me, but you are going to be sore for a long time yet."

Turan's cave was in the rocks on the other side of the sandy cove and could only be reached by flying over the sea. Rork had never been inside before, but he had heard lots of rumours about it and what he had heard about Turan was certainly strange.

The Admiral made a different sort of cry and Rork's two young cousins quickly flew down to join them. They immediately began to ask Rork questions, but the Admiral silenced them. "There'll be plenty of time for you to learn what has happened later," said the Admiral curtly. "I want you to help Rork get to Turan's cave so that she can treat his wound. He may need to rest on the way and he will need protecting."

The two young gulls nodded eagerly. They were flattered to have been asked to do such an adult task by the Admiral, particularly to help such an important gull as Rork.

"As soon as you've got him there safely, come back and meet me here to let me know. You can then help spread the word about the meeting tonight. We will hold it at the Town Roost at sunset."

Once again, Rork threw himself off the edge and into the unknown. This time, it was the edge of the harbour wall and he headed towards the waters of the sandy cove. He felt a little stronger and heartened by the encouraging words of his old leader. He managed to maintain reasonable height until halfway across the little bay, when exhaustion swept through him once more. He signalled to Faz and Jez that he was going down and he glided to a point just beyond the breaking surf where there did not seem to be any bathers. Faz and Jez alighted next to him and kept watch while Rork struggled to control his laboured breathing.

Rork looked about him in amazement at how normal everything seemed to be. The shrieks and laughter from the holidaymakers continued, the sun beat down out of an amazingly blue sky and the sea beneath him felt deliciously cool. Just then, he noticed two small boys in a yellow inflatable dinghy rowing erratically but purposefully towards him. The two young gulls noticed at the same time and made high-pitched shrieking calls while flapping their wings with as much vigour as they could muster. Rork smiled inwardly as the two small boys ignored their protestations and continued rowing towards them.

"Calm down lads! They won't hurt us. Just give me a few more moments to get my breath back and we will be on our way."

The two young boys had other ideas and even Rork was alarmed at how close they were getting. Jez flew down with his beak outstretched to attack the yellow plastic tubes of the inflatable in an effort to deflate them. To his great surprise, he rebounded off them and sat open-mouthed in the water while Faz laughed until he ached. The two boys rowed determinedly closer to Rork.

"This one is hurt!" cried one of the boys. "I can see blood on his chest and in the water."

"Come on Rork, we've got to go," squealed Faz. Rork desperately tried to paddle through the water to pick up speed and panted as he flapped his wings at the same time. Despite all his efforts, he failed to become unstuck and settled back on the water again. He tried to remember what he had been taught about taking off from water and he looked for a suitable wave to give him assistance.

Suddenly he felt two small hands gripping him gently and firmly over his wings and lifting him out of the water. "We'll take him to the RSPCA," said the youngster, convinced he was doing the right thing. Just then, the two young gulls swooped down and used their webbed feet to threaten the boy. The tactic worked; in his panic, the boy fell backwards in the dinghy, throwing Rork into the air as he did so. Rork seized the opportunity and, with his newfound fear, gained the energy to fly to the entrance of Turan's cave.

Still panting from these exertions, Rork grinned at his cousins. "Well done lads. You were both brilliant and very brave."

"I'll go and find someone to help you, " said Faz, to cover his embarrassment.

"Yes and I'll go and tell the Admiral that we made it," said Jez, glancing at his brother.

Rork smiled again at their kindness and watched them fly off. When they were out of sight, he stretched his wings in relief and let the sun soak into him.

The next thing Rork felt was someone shaking him gently by his outspread wing. Rork realised he must have momentarily fallen asleep. Opening his eyes, he imagined he had died and gone to heaven. Standing before him, silhouetted in the sunshine streaming into the entrance to the cave, Rork saw in shadow the most beautiful gull he had ever seen. She stepped a pace back and the sunlight lit her face. She was young, her feathers were completely white and she had the most perfect features that Rork could imagine.

"Hello Rork," she said. "My name is Dew. We have been expecting you. Do you think you can follow me into the cave? Turan is waiting to see you." With that, she turned and walked slowly into the darkness of the cave.

Rork followed as she twisted and turned along the rocky path of the cave floor. Several times she had to wait as Rork struggled over the uneven surface, but she did not embarrass him by trying to help. As they moved deeper into the cave, they walked beside a deep pool of water. Sunlight filtered down through holes in the cave roof. It was reflected by the water into strangely beautiful dapples and designs that moved and played on the rock walls. In some corners of the cavern, Rork noticed other gulls sitting or lying down, many of them seeming to be asleep.

During a pause in their progress, Rork asked, "Are they all injured? Were any of them hurt by the men too?"

Dew looked about her. "Most of the gulls here are old and cannot look after themselves. They come here because we can help them and treat their ailments. The more seriously ill and injured birds are together in one large chamber of the cave so we can give them more concentrated nursing. Just follow me around this corner and I will show you."

Rork followed her and immediately they came into the large chamber she described. It was high and so wide that the light did not reach into every corner. The floor was mainly flat and covered in clean and comfortable nesting materials. At evenly spaced intervals lay sick and seriously injured gulls. And again, many of them seemed to be asleep, or at least lay with their eyes closed. Dew led Rork to a corner in which there was fresh water and a small assortment of food to eat.

"You can help yourself to whatever is here in a moment. I'll show you to your bed and let Turan know you are here. She won't keep you waiting long – please under no circumstances keep her waiting. She is extremely busy and hates her time to be wasted."

Rork thanked her gratefully and settled where he was shown. Just minutes later, Dew returned with other gulls, led by the most diminutive and peculiar gull Rork had ever seen. By her very presence, Rork guessed that this must be the famous Turan herself. Renowned throughout the gull colony for her powers of healing, good works and dedication to duty, tales about Turan were legend. Rork recalled stories of her working in the aftermath of the Great Storm of 1987, so he knew she was a great age for a gull.

Turan's face was thin and gaunt and appeared to be bald in places. Her whole body was no bigger than that of a sparrow, but her movements were quick and sharp and full of a nervous energy. Her eyes were just black dots, yet they shone brightly and gazed piercingly at Rork. At Dew's request, Rork

9

described what had happened to him and showed Turan the wound in his chest. "You have been shot, my boy, from a gun. Good. We don't have many such injuries in here and it will do my colleagues a lot of good to see what damage has been done to you."

With that, Turan carefully parted the feathers around the wound to reveal a hole, black with dried blood. "You are obviously a very lucky gull, very lucky. The shot appears to be a single one that has ricocheted from a solid object – probably the piece of tin you talked about. That has taken a lot of the force out of it. Your second stroke of luck is that it has hit your breastbone squarely and not entered your lung. This may be painful, but it won't take long."

Without further ado, Turan dipped her tiny, sharp beak into some water and immediately dipped it into the hole in Rork's chest. As predicted, the pain was excruciating and Rorks eyes watered involuntarily. It was all he could do to stop himself crying out in pain and he probably would have done had it not been for the presence of the beautiful Dew. Rork knew that Turan was being as gentle as possible, but as he felt her beak probe inside him, he passed out in a dead faint.

Moments later he awoke and all but Dew had left his bedside.

"Well done Rork, you were very brave," said Dew. "Do you want to see what Turan found inside you? She was really triumphant! I haven't seen her that happy with a patient for a long time." Dew passed a hard black metal object for Rork to see. "I am going to clean your wound now. Again this is going to hurt I'm afraid, but not as much as Turan did because I will only touch the surface of the wound." With that, Dew set to work, gently and delicately and with great skill.

Rork quite enjoyed the attention she gave him and wondered whether she gave all her patients such wonderful care. As she tended him, Rork tried to find out more about her. He learned that she had been working in the cave hospital for almost five years and was now one of the senior nursing assistants. She lived in the cliffs nearby and obtained most of her food requirements from the farms at the top of the cliffs. Rork wanted desperately to ask her if she had a mate, but discretion got the better part of his valour. When the wound was cleaned to Dew's satisfaction, she turned her attention to the rest of him. Suddenly Rork realised how dishevelled and dirty he really was. He stuttered protestations that he could take care of these ablutions himself, but she pooh-poohed the idea and carried on preening and cleaning him. This was totally outside Rork's experience and his embarrassment was only matched by hers too when, as she carefully tended to Rork's face, they accidentally touched beaks.

"Turan will come back this evening to see how you are getting on," said Dew, suddenly flustered. "In the meantime please eat a little and drink a little and rest as much as you can."

"Oh, I won't be here this evening!" Rork sat up in alarm. "The Admiral has called for a public meeting at the town roost and I must be there to see what we can do to stop the men murdering our flock."

"Don't worry, Rork – she knows you have to be at the meeting as the Admiral has requested your presence. She will only stop you going if she thinks it will endanger your recovery. She will visit you in plenty of time to assess you and to let you get there."

As she said this, Dew smiled, and in that instant did more to aid Rork's recovery than any amount of medicines and ministrations would do. As she left, she promised to also see him later in the day.

It must have been mid-afternoon when Rork next awoke; he was surprised that he had slept for so long. He stretched and grimaced in pain as the bruising around the wound made its presence felt. As he turned, he was startled to see a gull staring down at him with a most quizzical expression. He had a round and kindly face, and if Rork had to guess, he would describe him as a bird of learning.

"I say old chap, did I wake you? I really am most dreadfully sorry."

"Please don't worry about it," said Rork, aware of his visitor's obvious discomfort. "I am surprised I have slept for so long."

"May I introduce myself?" The stranger went on. "My name is Barff and I help the Admiral with the pastoral side of the colony. He has asked me to visit you to get more details about the dreadful events you have witnessed. I'm afraid I'm going to have to ask you a lot of questions. Do you feel up to answering them?"

"Please feel free to ask as many questions as you like," said Rork, "I just hope I can help you, but don't see what I can add to what I have already told the Admiral."

"One of the things I'm afraid I'm going to need from you are the names of all the birds that were with you in the quarry this morning. I need to know which of them you saw being killed or wounded and therefore which of them there are still doubts about."

"I don't think there's much doubt that all the others died," said Rork bitterly. "I did not see any sign of anyone trying to follow me out of the quarry. Even if they were only wounded by these 'guns', as Turan called them, the big machinery would surely have finished them off as it flattened them and then buried them."

There was an awkward pause while both of them considered the enormity of this remark. The silence was broken by the approach of Dew. "Excuse me Rork, would you mind if I cleaned your wound again while you talk? I won't have much time later if you're going to go to the meeting."

Rork was relieved at the interruption and told Dew to carry on.

"I know it's not easy for you," said the kindly Barff," but my colleagues and I have got to visit each and every family of those that were there, and we will be questioned closely by the relatives as to what actually happened. We have to make these visits later this afternoon and break the sad news to the relatives before it is put in the public domain at the meeting."

Rork suddenly understood and apologised for his brusqueness. He looked at Barff in a new light and saw what a caring, thoughtful bird he was. Then he closed his eyes and began to recount the events of that morning from the moment he had woken up. He recalled meeting up with Vena and Dostin and the others, laughing and joking with them as they flew up over the Downs and sped down to the quarry to eat. When he got to the part of his story, where Vena was shot and all that was left of her was her unmarked wing, Rork again choked and spoke with a catch in his voice.

After he had finished, Barff asked gently, "Was Vena your partner?"

Dew's eyes widened as she overheard the question.

"No," replied Rork painfully. "Vena was like a mother to me. She brought me up from a chick. My mother died when I was just a few days old so I don't remember her. Vena didn't have chicks of her own but she brought me up as though I was hers. She was also great fun and a wonderful friend."

"I'm so sorry Rork," said Barff quietly. "I didn't mean to intrude, but I have to ask these things. I have a lot of families to see now. I'll leave you to rest and if you're up to it, I'll see you at the meeting tonight."

Chapter 2 – The Conspirators

All around the harbour ran a cobbled street, lined with quaint houses and businesses that had grown up to service the burgeoning tourist industry. The most impressive building, standing at the far end of the harbour opposite the harbour entrance, was the Victory Hotel and Public House. It had been a coaching inn long before the Battle of Trafalgar but had changed its name in the surge of patriotism and popularity for Nelson that followed his famous victory. Although it was only midday, its bars were already busy with happy holidaymakers seeking refreshment. The outside tables and chairs were particularly popular with those desperate to maintain a suntan while they ate, and the dishes of the day (beef and Guinness pie, a crab salad or freshly caught plaice with chips) were already in danger of selling out.

In the back of the pub, in a corner of the shaded courtyard, was a small snug bar where the landlord of the renowned establishment was serving some of his regular customers. He shakily set four pints of Dartmoor Bitter down on the bar and each was immediately accepted.

"There you are boys – three pints of foaming glory. Now do you deserve it? How many did you get this morning?"

"Shhhh Mike, for Christ's sake! Keep your voice down, we don't want everyone to hear."

"Don't panic Barry." Mike Frost gave his usual hurt look at the first hint of any criticism. The landlord indicated over his shoulder at the bar behind him. "No one will hear us above all the hubbub from in there."

Barry Clifton, the tallest of the three customers, wiped beer froth from his heavy moustache. The ale dripped down the side of his glass on to his brightly coloured tie, which projected over his huge beer belly. "We must have got about twelve I suppose." He dabbed his tie ineffectually with his handkerchief. "There weren't so many there today."

"It's no good then mate." The landlord's voice rose again. "We're not even making a dent in their numbers at this rate. Are you sure we can't apply for a licence and put a stop to all this secrecy?"

The pint glass was stopped just before it reached the moustache again. "I've told you before Mike, I will never get it granted. There are too many blooming do-gooders and animal lovers serving on the council for them to see it our way."

"Yeah 'n I bet they are mostly newcomers. Like that hippy Marjorie Whatserface and her New Age souvenirs shop. I don't understand them at all! The darned things are worse than rats in the damage they do." James Hawkes was the youngest of the four men present. His sharp features were set meanly above his thin mouth. He was the only one of the four wearing shorts, which sported many tatty pockets stuffed with the tools of his trade as a plumber.

"You're telling me. They are ruining my business," drawled Derek Marsden. He stopped lolling against the bar and looked disdainfully at his friend Barry's fat stomach. "It's bad enough in the winter when they defecate all over my cars and ruin the paint work, but I'm trying to sell sports cars and Cabriolets now, and you should see the mess it makes of the leather upholstery. It doesn't come off without a hell of a lot of work and even then it leaves a bleach mark." With a quick movement of his head, he flicked his long hair back into place and pouted his distaste.

"So why don't you leave the hoods up then, Derek?" James asked with a mischievous glint in his eye.

"Stop trying to wind me up, you horrible little manual worker." Derek gave James a good-natured cuff round the ear. "You know I hate it when you try to tell me my job. Cars sell better with the hoods down, and anyway, the hood material is just as hard to clean. Surely these people know how much work the beggars cause us?"

The landlord spoke again, deliberately not lowering his voice. "I'm sure if the council heard as many complaints each day from the newcomers as I get, then it would have to take action." He coughed heavily and patted his pockets for his cigarettes. "It's not just the mess they make; they are also getting far too daring when it comes to nicking food. The other day, one of them landed on a table when people were eating and was trying to get food from one of their plates. When they tried to shoo it away, it had the bloody cheek to try and peck one of them."

"Yeah, but let them find out that we're killing gulls and guess what they will say?" the councillor opined. "They come here on holiday and they love to hear the gulls in the morning and see them wheeling around in the sky. To them it's part of what being at the seaside is all about."

"You ask dear old Kipper Dobson whether gulls should be killed or not," said Derek affectedly. "He has to stay in his hut all day down at the car-park because every time he steps out to take ticket money, one of those dirty creatures attacks him. He reckons if it wasn't for his peaked cap he'd have been pecked to pieces."

"He's such a miserable old so and so, they are probably doing it to stop him moaning!" The landlord's chuckle at his own joke ended in a fit of coughing.

"Yeah but he'll tell you that the gulls used to be following the fishing fleet – when there was such a thing – and nesting in the cliff tops. Now they're everywhere and eating anything. I always thought it was the foxes attacking our bin bags, but the other morning I looked out and saw it was the gulls!"

16

"We need more guns…"

"We need a few better shots you mean," sneered the little man. "I think I got most of the birds this morning while all you two did was to scare yourselves!"

Derek looked at Barry Clifton and winked. The four of them had bantered like this over pints of beer for as long as any of them could remember. "You've just got a bloodlust, James. The gulls don't affect your plumbing business, do they?"

"They affect my missus though, don't they?" said James hotly. "And they cost me money. Instead of hanging the sheets from the B and B out to dry, Mrs Hawkes the First is sticking them in the tumble-drier because of the shit that was landing on them."

Mike Frost tried to keep the conversation serious. "Where else can we shoot them without the busybodies complaining?"

Councillor Clifton was quick to answer him. "There *is* nowhere else where we can hide the evidence as easily. If they found out what we are doing they'd have the RSPB down on us like a ton of bricks."

Suddenly a fresh voice called out from the open doorway of the bar. "I might have known it! I guessed I should find you lot in here. Nothing changes in this little place, does it?"

"Good lord! Dear oh dearie me, look what the wind's blown in!" Mike Frost said this more loudly than ever. He took his hands off the bar, wiped the right one on his shirt front and held it out to greet his latest visitor. "Bryan Jordan, as I live and breathe. How the devil are you, boy?"

The new visitor took the proffered hand and shook it warmly. "I'm good, thank you very much, and how are all of you?" He looked round at the other three and shook their hands too. He patted his stomach and smiled. "You look as though you are all living very well!"

"Don't include me when you're making that insinuation," sneered James Hawkes. "*I* haven't put on any weight since I last saw you."

"Don't tell me!" said Bryan Jordan. "You've given up the evil booze because you can't afford it. You're just in here to collect for the missionaries!"

"Something like that," agreed James with a grin.

"Come off it, who do you think you're kidding? I didn't have to think very hard to know where I would find you lot at this time of day." Bryan Jordan's white teeth flashed against his very suntanned face as he smiled broadly at the others.

"Come on Mike, pull us a pint for God's sake!"

"It's very good to see you, Mr. Jordan. What brings such an important man as you to our humble world?" Derek Marsden felt the quality of Bryan Jordan's shirt appreciatively. "You've not come here for your clothes shopping, that's for sure!"

"You all know why I've come here, boys. I've just come to make the final preparations for Saturday."

"Saturday? What's happening on Saturday? Anything important?" Mike winked at Barry and James.

"Oh, it's the start of the football season isn't it? Of course, we're all going to watch Plymouth's opening match, aren't we?" James kept a straight face as he said this.

"I'm not sure I can," said Derek. "I've got to go and look at a car in Taunton."

"That's all right. I assume your invitations went astray and that you want to miss out on the best bash that this little town has ever seen. Champagne, caviar, live music and some of the tastiest totty you lot are ever likely to see!"

"So we don't *have* to bring our wives along then? There will be plenty of spare women for us?" Mike Frost said this half seriously.

"Oh, so you *are* coming. Sorry guys, I'm afraid that bringing your better halves is obligatory. Erica is looking forward to seeing them all again and getting updated with all the gossip."

"Jeez Bryan, you just try and stop them! They have been

18

talking about little else for months now. What to wear, what the weather's going to be like, what to wear, who'll be there, what to wear…"

"Yeah! You're costing us all a fortune." moaned the little man.

Mike Frost placed a tall glass of lager on the counter in front of Bryan Jordan. "When will the boat be here, Bryan?"

"We are hoping to bring her in tomorrow, about half an hour before high water." Bryan sipped his lager appreciatively. "It's going to be touch and go – literally – as to whether we make it. She draws about a foot less than the predicted depth in the harbour at this time of year. We've just been out in a RIB taking soundings and it seems OK. Fingers crossed!"

"The whole town is talking about you, you know that don't you?" Derek Marsden had a touch of envy in his voice. "They all want to see this great big yacht of yours. The word on the street is that drug smuggling is paying better than ever these days."

Bryan Jordan pulled a face. "Not that old chestnut, please! Do you mean to say that is still being said about us?"

Barry Clifton put an affectionate arm around Bryan's shoulder. "They only say it in fun, Bryan. It's just natural jealousy, that's all."

"I know that," said Bryan. "But it does get rather wearying in the end. What have you lot been up to lately? What were you plotting when I came in?"

"Nothing, old boy," said Derek Marsden quickly. "We were just talking about you and in you came, large as life."

"Yeah, talking about life, some of us have got to get on with it and do some *real* work around here." James downed the last of his pint and set the glass down on the bar. "I'll see you on Saturday evening, Bryan, and I'll see the rest of you tomorrow morning."

Chapter 3 – The Town Roost Meeting

Rork flew with Dew to the edge of the roost and landed on a ledge behind a group of chimneys. He had made it from the cave in one flight, but when he landed his breath was laboured and he did not want to be seen puffing and panting by the other birds that were already gathered. While he collected himself, Dew looked around and said, "Listen to them Rork. They are excited about the meeting but they don't know why it has been called."

Rork listened to the noisy but muted chattering of the gull colony. The town roost was on the roof of Barlmouth town hall and the surrounding council buildings. These were mainly Victorian Gothic edifices that had been constructed in the heyday of Barlmouth in the late 19th century. At that time, it was a thriving and busy fishing port with over thirty vessels making a successful living from the industry. There was an important twice-weekly market for the surrounding farms and villages. It had also become an extremely popular and fashionable resort for the West Country gentry who wished to practice the new craze for sea bathing. They arrived there in their thousands on the newly opened branch line of the Great Western Railway. Barlmouth's importance was recognised when it was granted county borough powers in the late 1880s and earned its independence from the county council. To celebrate its newfound status and to reinforce its authority, the new council had immediately commissioned the building of the new town hall.

As Rork and Dew stepped around the corner of the

chimney, the sight that met their eyes astounded both of them. Gulls were crowded into every conceivable corner of roof space, and the braver were perched on ridges and chimneys to get the best view of the meeting. Anticipation was running high and Rork could hear snatches of their conversations as they tried to guess the subject of the meeting. "… Perhaps The Admiral is going to retire…" said one. "No," said his friend, "it's more important than that. Something's up – you mark my word."

As Rork and Dew threaded their way through the throng, they greeted those they knew and nodded to other acquaintances. The murmurings became more subdued and Rork realised that some of them knew he was involved. "Oh look, there he is… he don't look too bad to me …"he heard one of them utter.

Roughly in the centre of the roof space was a large rectangular structure about two feet high consisting mainly of glass. It was the skylight above the main council chamber itself. In an effort to prevent birds landing on it and defacing it with their droppings, the council had covered it with a wire mesh. This had long since become dilapidated and now was merely used as a means of grip for the gulls as they roosted. This space was largely empty and in the centre stood the friendly figure of Barff. Rork was pleased to see his kindly round face again. Barff beckoned and Rork and Dew hopped onto the skylight.

"Hello old chap, it's good to see you again. You certainly seem a lot better than the last time we met. They must have done a very good job on you."

"They certainly did," said Rork, glancing gratefully at Dew." They were extremely kind and very clever. I'm beginning to feel more my old self." Beside Barff, a serious-looking gull was listening intently to what they were saying. He was tall and rather lean for a gull, which only accentuated his height. He had to stoop to listen to Barff.

Barff introduced Rork and Dew to the imposing gull. "I'd

like you to meet Ardyl. Ardyl is here to advise us what to do."

"I'm glad you could make it. You are very lucky to do so by all accounts." Rork agreed and turned back to Barff, who introduced Rork to other birds around him. Rork realised that they were all leaders in one form or another. Each of them greeted Rork warmly and congratulated him on his survival. Before Rork could adequately reply, a hush fell upon the gathered crowd as the huge presence of the Admiral took centre stage.

He stood erect and proud and stared about him, quelling the last of the whisperers with his single black beady eye.

"Thank you all for coming," said the Admiral tersely. "I know it was short notice, but as you will learn, it is very important. I'm sorry that we have to break some bad news to you. This morning one of our numbers witnessed an atrocity that concerns us all. He was badly wounded in the attack himself, but because of his courage and his strength of mind and body, he has survived to tell his tale to us all."

Rork bowed his head and shuffled his feet in utter embarrassment as the Admiral said these words.

"As you may now realise, some of our numbers were killed in the atrocity and their close families have been informed. However, this may come as a tremendous shock to many others of you who were their friends and neighbours. And now I want to hand over to Rork, whom I am sure many of you know already, so he can relate to you what he witnessed in his own words."

Rork glanced at Dew, a horrified expression on his face. "I didn't realise I'd be asked do this," he hissed.

"You'll be fine," said Dew reassuringly, "if you tell it as you saw it, it will help them understand."

Rork took heart from that and walked forward to the edge of the skylight. The other gulls left a space around him. The silence was profound. He started hesitantly, but recounted in a clear voice how that very morning (was it really that very morning – it all seemed a lifetime ago) he and the others had flown to the landfill site. He almost choked when he recounted the death of his best friend, but he recovered himself just in time. The majority of the gulls listened in shocked silence without any interruption, save for the anguished cries of the relatives when they heard the names of their loved ones mentioned, only to realise they were dead.

"… And then I woke up to hear the big machines coming towards me and knew that I had to get back to tell the Admiral what had happened…"

"What Rork is not telling you is the tremendous effort he made to overcome his own injuries; and to fly out of the quarry and over the Downs to reach me," said the Admiral. "We owe him a debt of gratitude."

"We owe the devils that did this another sort of debt too!" cried a voice from the darkness of one of the chimneys.

"Yeah, we've got to get them back for what they did," cried another.

"If they did this to us today, how many times have they done it before and got away with it?" called another.

The clamour rose, with demands for vengeance and the questions about missing relatives intertwined. Shouts were heard from all parts of the roost, with most birds on their feet, all of them trying to speak at once. The Admiral spread his wings to get attention and to try and silence the furore, but it did not die down for quite a few moments, even for him.

"I know you are all angry. I know you have many questions. I know you will want us to take some form of action. That is why we have called a meeting. Please try and restrain yourself so we can hear one voice at time. Who is going to be first to speak?" The Admiral looked at the roof ridge to his right where a particularly vociferous group was perched.

"Torg, I know that you will want to say something. Please be first."

The bird that the Admiral was addressing was a small but wiry-looking creature with a hard and careworn face. He looked fiercely about him as if daring others to interrupt.

"Admiral, do you agree that for some time I have been saying that dark forces were at work and taking some of us away?"

Ardyl cut in before the Admiral had a chance to reply. "Torg, I agree that we have spoken about this before, but this is the first time that any proof of wrongdoing has been provided to us."

"So you have done absolutely nothing to protect us? You've just let this happen?" barked Torg furiously.

"I'd admit that we do seem to have had more than the usual numbers of missing gulls," replied Ardyl carefully. "And we have looked into each individual case very carefully to see if we can find out the reason for the disappearance of one of us, but in each case we have not found any satisfactory explanation."

"Just how many disappearances have you investigated, and just how many does it take for you to investigate before you let the rest of us know that something is seriously wrong?" demanded Torg. The crowd sensed the sneering tone in his voice and murmured in agreement.

Ardyl looked awkwardly at the Admiral, who nodded imperceptibly in reply.

"We have probably investigated over 150 disappearances." The noise from the crowd rose up more angrily from this disclosure by Ardyl. "We first started noticing something was wrong in mid-winter. This is not the normal time gulls move on to fresh areas, and although our numbers do get reduced by natural causes more in the wintertime, it seemed that higher numbers than usual were missing."

"I came to you because my brother and sister were both missing," said Torg. "Are you telling me that you had no idea at all what had happened to them?"

24

It was obvious to the other gulls that the questioning by Torg was making those on the skylight feel very awkward and they were happy at this stage to leave the questioning to him.

This time it was Barff's turn to reply. "We knew that it was not just the very young or very old gulls that were disappearing. Nor was it the single and the more adventurous amongst you. Although we suspected that something was happening, we could not figure it out because there were no illnesses or accidents reported more than usual."

"And is that as far as you have got with your *investigations*?" Torg did not try to hide the derision in his voice and the stress on the last word.

"The only common factor was that the disappearances happened to birds who were working farthest away from the colony. We were intending to send observers to the farms, to the fishing fleet and to the landfill site when Rork came back with his dreadful news."

Another big and very tough-looking gull named Krom stood up and flapped his wings angrily. "Just how many of us were you going to let get killed before you warned the rest of us what was happening?"

Barff shifted his feet uncomfortably. Seeing his plight, the Admiral stepped in.

"If no evidence of wrongdoing had been found by our observers, it had been our intention to put out a general warning without causing too much alarm."

"Given that you have had longer to think about this than we have," said Torg, "how do you propose we stop this happening and get revenge for our dead relatives?"

Ardyl stepped forward to field the question. "This is a very difficult subject for any of us to answer. There are many more men than us, so it is difficult to fight them all. They are also bigger than us and they have learned to use machines."

"So you're saying what exactly... Do nothing?"

From another section of roof came the voice of a female gull. "If we did try to wage war against human beings they would surely kill us all!"

Another female voice from the same section called out in agreement. "I've already lost one son to them; I don't want to lose my others to them in the same way."

"But that is just the damned point," declaimed Torg, "they are killing us anyway! If they have killed over 150 of us in the last few months, there won't be any of us left to fight them soon."

"Yeah, and then they'll be able to wipe us out completely."

"Of course we got to fight the beggars. They've left us no choice." The last speaker seemed to sway the majority of those present on the roof. There was a general roar of approval that echoed around the streets with many of them calling out in agreement."

To Rork's utter amazement, Dew stepped forward. "There *has* to be an alternative to war," she said in a clear ringing voice. "Surely history has shown all of us that nothing can be gained by going to war. Although these are horrific things that man has done to us, we can't really contemplate the finality of going to war when we haven't even considered peaceful alternatives."

This simple statement produced another cheer from a mainly female section of gulls, albeit not as vociferous or angry as the one from those favouring violence.

"What do you suggest then?" said Torg sarcastically. "A protest march with each of us holding up white feathers?"

Dew stepped back with a crestfallen look on her face. Krom flew down onto the skylight and turned to face Ardyl. Krom easily matched Ardyl in height, but his muscular frame made Ardyll appear frail in comparison. Both stretched their necks to the utmost and stood beak to beak, glaring at each other.

"Yes, of course there are more of them than us. Yes, of course they are bigger than us and I know they've got machines. But the swines can't fly can they? We've got to attack them and peck their blasted eyes out!"

Krom's words met with raucous cries of approval from all around the roost. Ardyl stood his ground and continued to stare angrily at Krom. Just for a split second, Rork thought a fight may break out between them.

Again, Dew stepped forward and placed herself just by the vying pair. "I'm sure that fighting amongst ourselves would bring great satisfaction to the people who are doing this to us." Her words were largely drowned by the continuing clamour for vengeance.

"For pity's sake, give her a chance to speak," someone shrieked from the back of the crowd. "Surely we can't let them reduce us to savages?" The caller had taken advantage of a lull in the shouting and her appeal seemed to do the trick. This gave Dew the courage to continue.

"There is of course one very simple thing we can do to stop the killing. We can stop feeding at the landfill site."

The suggestion brought about a degree of quiet while the birds muttered to each other and considered its implications.

"Why are they just choosing to kill us while we feed in the quarry?" asked a small gull sitting off to Rork's left. "Surely we are only feeding on rubbish that they have thrown away, so why do they want to kill us for it?"

Rork stepped forward. "There is a very simple explanation for that, although it took me a great deal of thinking before I realised what it was," he replied. "The men are not trying to protect the rubbish they have thrown away. They just see the landfill site as the most convenient place to destroy us. Not only are we an easy target there, but also they can quickly cover the bodies of the gulls they kill and in doing so hide the evidence of their murderous deed." He looked down at Dew by his side. "I'm sorry, but I can't agree with the last speaker. If we stopped feeding at the quarry they would simply find us at another place and do the evil deed there instead. As I see it, we are left with no alternative but to protest in the strongest possible way to show them this is utterly unacceptable, and if this has no effect – in other words, if they continue in their efforts to kill us – then we have to wage war against them or face extinction!"

Dew glared furiously at Rork and moved away from him, sending a very clear message. However, Rork's words again brought about a roar from the majority of those present at the meeting. "What we waiting for – more deaths? Let's kill them now!"

The Admiral sensed the rebellion in the crowd was gaining the upper hand and again stepped forward with his wings outstretched in a gesture of peace and in an attempt to get quiet. Such was the respect that he commanded, he eventually managed to subdue the angry meeting but those near to him could see that he was angry as well.

"I am shocked and dismayed by the bad language and behaviour of some of you!" He turned and glared at Krom as he said this. "If you are not going to debate this in a civilised and proper manner, then you can look for another leader because I shall have absolutely nothing further to do with it."

He paused to let these dramatic words have their effect, which they did almost immediately. Krom backed down at the implied challenge.

"I am sorry, Admiral. I did not mean to lose my temper, but we cannot stand by and let these murderers get away with it."

"Krom is right. We cannot and shall not stand by and let them get away with it." The Admiral's tone of voice was conciliatory. "He is also right when he points out that humans cannot fly. That is the key for us. And we shall use our flying skills to show the men that we are not prepared to let them do this to us. But we must first try and do this without violence. Allow us to devise a plan of action to make such a protest clear before we try to hurt the humans and before they kill any more of us."

Ardyl took the lead that the Admiral had shown. "We will need the very best fliers among you to carry this out. Any birds wishing to volunteer for active service please report to me and my colleagues after the meeting."

"If everyone agrees to let us have this day of action, then I suggest the meeting is closed," said the Admiral feeling a great sense of relief.

Torg also flew down and turn to address the crowd. "Krom and I will be the first to volunteer for you. We will give your day of protest the best we have got. But mark my words…" Torg's voice rose to a shrill crescendo, "… if it doesn't work we will soon do something about it."

"That is a bloody sell-out and you know it, Torg!" cried one of the gulls that Torg had been sitting with. "We want to avenge our relatives, not to play stupid war games!"

Torg looked up towards the source of the voice. "Remember that they were my brother and sister too, Steg. I think you know I'm no coward and if this does not work I'll be the first to find another way."

This consensus seemed to appease all sides of the argument, and the meeting gradually broke up. Gulls of all ages, shapes and sizes came forward to volunteer. Ardyl turned to Krom. "I want you to lead what we shall call the heavy brigade and train them in what to do. Get the names of the largest birds you can find and work with them tomorrow. Train them to work together as a unit and accept discipline. Don't let up until you are totally happy with them. When you are satisfied with their progress, ask them to come to a briefing here tomorrow night." He then turned to Torg.

"Torg, I want you to pick the fastest and most agile flyers you can find. They will need to be brave and quick thinking too. I need you to test them for these qualities and train them tomorrow and then report with them tomorrow night at a briefing too."

Rork joined one of the queues to register his willingness

to fly. Dew tugged angrily at his shoulder. "Rork, you cannot volunteer to help just yet. You are too weak still and your body will not take it."

Rork smiled kindly at her and spoke gently but firmly. "I have to do this, Dew. I have to do this for Slet and Dostin and Vena and all the others who have died."

"That stupid macho attitude will get you and all the others killed too." Dew spoke in a low voice but every syllable carried the strength of her feeling. "If you must be so immature, then please see you get a good rest tomorrow instead of wearing yourself out playing soldiers. Please report to the hospital in the morning and the afternoon to have your wound cleaned."

With that, she turned quickly around and flew away, leaving Rork feeling confused and angry with himself.

Chapter 4 – Next Day, Back in the Snug...

"Three pints and whatever you're having please Mike."
Derek Marsden hung his carefully crumpled linen jacket over
a nearby chair. "It's so flipping hot out there. I hope you've
got enough beer in for the weekend because at this rate you
are going to need double the normal week's worth."

Just as he said this, James Hawkes walked in wearing his
overalls with no shirt underneath. He was closely followed by
Barry Clifton.

"What a waste of a damned morning that was," said the
plumber. "Oh, cheers Derek. Which one's mine?"

The landlord passed a pint glass to the little plumber.
"Don't tell me you had a bad morning at the dump," he said.
"How many did you get today?"

The councillor sucked at the beer on his moustache. "We
didn't get any today, Mike. None of the little beggers showed
up."

"What, none of them?"

"Not one. It was most peculiar. There was a lot of food
scraps dumped there as well," continued the councillor.
"There were quite a few of the usual crows and magpies
feeding away but not one gull came down to have a go."

Derek ignored the no-smoking sign by his elbow, lit a
cigarette and drew deeply. "The gulls were there in the sky
above us wheeling around like they knew the food was there
all right but they didn't land."

"So why didn't you shoot them in the air?"

"Because they were flying far too high – and anyway, they

31

weren't flying over the landfill site but just staying slightly off it. It was just like they were watching us and waiting for us to go."

The men thought about this comment for a few moments and then the councillor said, "Perhaps they were. Perhaps they are learning what we are doing there and as soon as our backs are turned, they are dropping down to feed as normal. If that is the case then we will have to rig some sort of hide to conceal ourselves."

"And that'd be no good anyway," said James. "It would narrow our field of fire too much and only give us a chance to bag a couple of birds each at most."

"I wish they *were* learning," said the publican earnestly. "If they did learn to stay away from the tourists we wouldn't have to kill any more."

"Just think of yourself, why don't you?" spluttered Derek into his beer. "What about my car lot?"

But the publican ignored this remark and continued, "Do you know what? The birds have been behaving peculiarly here today too. They've been doing the usual diving down and grabbing whatever food they can, but they have also been flying overhead in large numbers and it almost seems as if they were in a formation."

"Perhaps they are getting ready before migration," said Derek hastily and then instantly regretted his remark.

"Act your age and not your shoe size," said the little plumber, causing the others to laugh. "For a start, our gulls don't migrate…"

"…And even if they did, they wouldn't do it in the middle of summer!" finished off the councillor in a fit of laughter.

"All right. All right. But if Mike's right, why have they been flying in formation?"

Mike bristled indignantly. "What d'you mean, 'If Mike's right?' I saw it with my own eyes – you ask anyone in town today what they saw." He stomped outside and looked up at the bright blue sky. It took a little time for his eyes to adjust from the darkness of the bar to the bright sunlight but then he saw them.

"Just come here and look at this," he cried. "You just try and explain this then."

The others joined him outside and looked to where he was pointing. Barry took his spectacles from his shirt pocket and Derek went back in the bar to get his sunglasses from his jacket pocket. Looking up, they saw a sight that was new to all of them. The area of sky that they could see from the courtyard was not particularly big. To one side, about 20 large gulls were flying in a line abreast. Behind them, perhaps another 15 were flying in a neat V formation. They turned their heads and looked above the other side of the pub courtyard where probably 30 gulls flew in a ragged square.

"Well, I'll go to the foot of our stairs," said the plumber in shock, "I've never seen gulls fly like that before. They are behaving more like ducks or geese."

"Yeah, I agree James," said the landlord, "but have you ever seen ducks or geese flying in a square formation?"

"I think that's just coincidence," said Derek. "They don't normally fly like that." As he spoke, they watched a single gull flying along a side of the square. It flew closely to where the line was most ragged. The birds here quickly drew into line and the square became defined again.

"Did you see that? Did you see that?" repeated James in amazement. "That bird on the outside is telling them to keep in line!"

They watched for a little while longer and then went back into the snug bar to finish their pints of bitter.

"So what are we going to do about meeting tomorrow?" asked the landlord.

The councillor scratched his head. "Perhaps we should change our time each day if they have recognised what we're doing and when we're doing it."

"Count me out then," said Derek instantly. "I can't leave the cars during the day in case I get a customer. There are so many visitors, and with this weather business is really good. Christ, it needs to be after last winter!"

"Yeah, we're not all like you," agreed the little plumber. "I need to earn a living and work every hour I can."

"My heart bleeds for you," grinned Barry. "All right. We'll meet at the usual time at the landfill site and see how things go."

Chapter 5 – Practice Makes Perfect

Rork woke later than normal as his night had been disturbed by the excited chitter-chattering of the gulls around him. A lot of it was nervous banter and Rork realised that most of the colony was facing the future with some trepidation. He had finally got to sleep as daylight was breaking and most of the colony had already gone about their daily business by the time he roused himself. He could still feel the bruising in his chest that spread from his breastbone through his ribcage, but it was already nowhere near as sore as the previous day. After a quick preening and a seafood breakfast from the nearest part of the shoreline, Rork flew to the top of Potton Hill to see what was happening.

He found Ardyl and Krom perched on a lamp standard that overlooked a small roundabout where the coast road met the main road into Barlmouth. Both birds seemed pleased to allow Rork to join them. Their gulls were circling overhead or feeding in nearby fields.

"My gulls are the ones in the air," explained Ardyl. "You're just about to see our first mock attack. Do you see the bus shelter over there? They're going to attack it without using live ammunition at this stage, just to see what problems we get."

With that, Ardyl let out a piercing shriek and the gulls in the air all swooped towards the bus shelter. As they approached within twenty bird lengths of the shelter, mayhem ensued. The first birds to reach the shelter pretended to release their cargo but instead of moving out of the way, they decided to hover and watch their colleagues come in for the kill. The larger and braver of them battered their way through the throng to complete their bombing run but the more cautious stalled in the air above the shelter until they saw a space to fill. Krom rocked with laughter but Ardyl was not amused.

"Chaos. Absolute blooming chaos! We certainly can't let them do that again. They have to get themselves into some sort of order." Ardyl let out another piercing screech but had to repeat it several times before he got the attention of all his flock. He instructed them to gather on the ground beyond the area where most footpaths criss-crossed. "Krom, go and have a few words with your chaps. Get them to come in from one direction and to fly off to a safe distance before they turn and watch. If we ever reach the stage where we are flying towards men with guns, they will slaughter us if we repeat that mistake."

Krom nodded his agreement and launched his huge body into the air to join his flock in the fields. Rork and Ardyl watched from the lamppost as they quickly gathered around him.

"I think he's going to make a good leader," said Ardyl thoughtfully. "He certainly won't tolerate any nonsense from any of them. I have asked around and Krom has the reputation for great strength and being good at fighting, but it seems he is not a bully. You can see he is already building some respect."

Krom's flock now took to the air and gained height, possibly too much, thought Rork. They swung out and over the cliffs and came back together towards the bus shelter. Krom was in the lead and dived steeply towards the 'target'. Some of the birds following vied for position and there were a number of collisions that caused a certain amount of friendly cursing. As they came near to the bus shelter, their proximity to each other became closer too and the amount of collisions increased. Because of the height and angle of attack, their speed was too great and some of the contacts made Rork clench his beak in sympathy. However, the attack was altogether swifter than the one made by Ardyl's birds, and Krom seemed pleased as he alighted back on the lamp standard. He looked at Ardyl expectantly.

"That was altogether a much better run than my lot made, Krom. What do you think?"

Rork admired Ardyl's handling of Krom. Rather than criticising or berating him, he was treating him as an equal partner and developing a strategy with him.

"Our angle of attack was all wrong. We came in too steep and therefore too fast and it caused some bumping and barging. The guys were more concerned with keeping out of each other's way than looking at the target and considering dropping their bombs."

This admission pleased Ardyl. "Exactly what I was thinking, Krom. I think we have to consider what target we are attacking and work out the best way of approaching it before we go in. We then need to tell them what to do and expect them to do it quickly. For instance, if you look at the bus shelter that we are practising on, there is no room for more than four gulls to attack it at once. Therefore, if we get the gulls to fly four abreast with a decent space between each row, each bird has more chance of a decent shot at the target."

Krom considered this for a moment. "That's an excellent suggestion, Ardyl. If we can get them to fly like that automatically and they come to do it naturally, they are not going to spend time thinking about flying – just thinking about how they are going to deliver their little message!"

"I'll go down to my lot and try and explain it to them. We'll have a bash at doing it again, but no laughing this time." Ardyl swooped away but Krom could not help calling out after him.

"Sorry, I can't guarantee that!"

Rork and Krom watched as Ardyl gathered his troops around him. After a few minutes, they saw Ardyl's birds line up in fours, still on the ground.

"This I've got to see," said Rork in amazement. "He's going to try to get them to take off in fours. Krom, why don't you get your chaps in the air so they can watch? They might learn how not to do it!"

"Good thinking again, Rork," laughed Krom, and flew off to organise his flock.

Suddenly Rork thought of Dew and the mood in which she had flown off last night. He knew that he should get to the hospital for his wound to be cleaned. He hoped that he could use the opportunity to be able to speak to Dew to somehow make things better between them. He was surprised to find himself caring like this, but he knew that he wanted her friendship more than anything he had wanted for a long time. However, he couldn't resist waiting until Ardyls birds had performed their second mock attack on the bus shelter. Their attempt to take off in a formation of four abreast did not go too well. The call that got them to go could not have been heard clearly by all the birds at once. Take-off was therefore sporadic, to say the least. Several collisions occurred and Rork could clearly hear loud cries of anger and frustration. He could also hear Krom's birds shriek with laughter as they watched.

Ardyl did his best to get them into line once they were in the air. When they were flying in a straight line, they seemed to manage to hold station with each other without too much difficulty, but when it came to a change of direction the formation began to disintegrate. The birds on the inside of the turn bunched up too close to each other to fly properly and the birds on the outside easily lost contact with the bird in front as they desperately tried to fly faster and faster to cover the extra distance required. In the end, Ardyl led them a good distance away and brought them back in a slow, very gradual turn. They managed to get into a reasonable shape by the time they reached the shelter and Rork thought their height was about right. Ardyl led them in mock attack and his idea seemed to work reasonably well. The leading birds got well out of the way before turning to watch, allowing the last of the flock space to enter the dropping zone. When the manoeuvre was completed, a loud cheer from Krom's birds greeted it and both groups flew to a nearby field to eat together. Ardyl and Krom flew back to join Rork on the lamppost.

"Well done Ardyl, that was excellent," Rork enthused. "If both your teams improve at this rate, by the end of the day they will be flying with an accuracy that no other flocks of birds have achieved before."

"Thanks Rork, it's nice to get some praise." Ardyl said this with an amused tone and looked at Krom meaningfully as he did so. "We have an awful lot to learn as you can see, particularly when it comes to a change of direction or height. The next go by Krom's lot should be interesting to watch as they are going to use 'live' ammunition. I've already warned them to watch their language!"

"I'm sorry I can't stick around to see it," said Rork meaning it. "I've been ordered to go to the hospital to have my wound cleaned twice, this morning and this afternoon, but I will try and get back to see some more."

"Oh, I don't suppose you'll be bumping into that gorgeous little nurse of yours by any chance will you?" Krom winked at Ardyl as he said this. Rork found himself embarrassed and stuck for words for once. He was not helped by the silence that ensued and the knowing grins exchanged by the other two.

"Actually, she's not *my* little nurse, but if I'm honest, I rather wish she were. I'll see you later this afternoon." Before Krom and Ardyl had the opportunity to reply, he was gone.

At Turan's cave, Rork's wish to see Dew and to make amends for their falling out found him sorely disappointed. Dew sent other nurses to examine him and attend to his wound. Whenever he did catch a glimpse of her, it was only to see her swiftly turn her back and walk in another direction. She obviously did not want to speak to him. He was unable to think of a suitable message to pass on to her and he left feeling thoroughly miserable. He could not face any more ribald comments from Krom and Ardyl so he went in search of Torg and his ground attack forces. In his first search, he was unable to see any sign of them, so he used the excuse to exercise and fly as high as he could. Rork loved to fly high, and in order to save energy he chose the area seaward of Potton Hill where the land stopped suddenly in a high white cliff. The cooler sea breeze hit the cliffs and created the most marvellous uplift when it met the warmth of the air over the land. Rork used all his experience to climb in wide circles until he could see probably 30 miles in each direction along the coast. On beautiful days such as this, he would normally soar for hours in perfect contentment, but today he felt sad and somewhat resentful.

From his great height, he could make out movement of the birds with Ardyl and Krom but he was too high to see any other gulls individually or otherwise. He relaxed his muscles and circled ever lower this time, unappreciative of the panorama before him. He had almost given up searching when he saw a splash at the foot of the cliffs and knew it was a seabird of some sort entering the water. He flew down and found where Torg was training his troops. Torg seemed totally absorbed in the task of teaching his birds, so Rork settled himself on the edge of the cliff halfway down where he had a good view in all directions.

Rork was astonished as he watched Torg put the faster and more agile gulls through their paces. He was pleased to see that Faz and Jez were among them, but he was also concerned that they would be too young to do what Torg expected of them. Torg's main strategy this afternoon appeared to be to test the bravery of each gull. He seemed to be asking them to fly to the top of the cliff and to dive at full speed, aiming at a small semi-submerged rock probably 200 ft below. The challenge seemed to be to touch the water over the rock just as they were pulling out of the dive. There were some gulls that did not quite have the nerve to achieve this and Torg separated them into a group of their own. There were others who misjudged when to pull out of the dive and in their over zealousness actually penetrated the water to strike the rock. That was what Rork had seen. Torg separated this smaller number into another group where many of them sat rubbing their bills ruefully. Rork watched for most of the afternoon as the successful ones practised again and again while the other two groups watched. Rork was extremely proud to see that his two young cousins were among them. Later in the afternoon, Torg split the good ones up amongst the two groups for further training, with each 'qualified' flyer taking two trainees for further tuition. Faz and Jez made Rork even more proud when he saw the care and the enthusiasm they put into training their charges.

When Torg called a halt to the afternoon's training, Rork was exhausted from merely watching! He could only imagine how tired the others must be. He sought Torg out and made a point of speaking to him and praising him on his training methods, particularly where he had used the more able birds to help the less able. Torg appreciated his comments. "I've divided them all into pairs and with each pairing I have put a top flyer as leader. In this way, the other flyer can benefit from his leader's judgment and they can both watch out for each other. I thought it unfair to send birds in to attack on their own because if something happened to them, there would be no one there to help." Rork admired the logic of Torg's thinking and, having said as much, he made his goodbyes and turned towards the hospital cave once more.

This time he was lucky enough to see Turan in person, who pronounced herself pleased with his progress. She then surprised Rork by dismissing her small entourage in order to speak privately with him.

"I don't know what you have heard about me, Rork. Have

41

you heard that I have mystical powers?" The question was merely rhetorical as Turan went on before Rork had chance to shape his reply. "They say I have a strange gift of healing, but that is a ridiculous rumour. All the work we do here is just good nursing practice, bound up with a great deal of common sense. This helps many to recover from their ailments, or at least learn to live with them more comfortably." She paused and Rork tried to interpose by praising his own treatment in her charge. She waved her wing dismissively and went on.

"I do however seem to have a small ability that sometimes turns into a weight that is heavy to carry." As she said this, her beady black eyes sparkled with a ferocity that bored into Rork's eyes as sharp as a gimlet. "I occasionally get a glimpse into the future and one such glimpse came to me as I slept last night. It wasn't a vision, nor was it a dream." This was said in such confidential tones that Rork was left in awe that Turan would share this with him and so he did not speak. "Our colony is threatened as never before in its history. I feel much destruction will follow. You, Rork, will find yourself burdened with an enormous responsibility. You must not try to shirk this duty, nor allow self-doubt to dilute your resolve. Your judgement will be tested to the core." With that, Turan swept out of the cave.

Rork stayed rooted to the spot for a few moments, transfixed by her enigmatic speech. All sorts of questions flooded into his brain that he would love to have put to Turan. What responsibility would he have to carry? What duty? Why him? He stirred himself and went in search of Dew. To his chagrin, he was unable to speak to her as she repeated her behaviour of the morning by busying herself in another direction as he approached. Feeling disappointed and frustrated at his inability to say anything to her, and thoroughly bewildered by his caution from Turan, Rork flew off to get some nourishment before the briefing.

Chapter 6 – The Briefing

Rork made sure he arrived in good time for the briefing. All the gulls that had volunteered for training were there, chattering excitedly with each other. Rork chose a spot close to a large and very dirty window. In the dirt, someone had drawn a reasonably accurate outline of the harbour and the small cove and the main roads of the town, showing where the River Barl cut through the hills to the harbour. Even the largest and most important buildings were marked with different sized squares.

Just as the last rays of the red setting sun were squeezed below the horizon, Barff flew down and landed next to Rork. At the same time, the Admiral arrived with some other gulls. Amongst them Rork saw Ardyl and recognised some of the other birds from the previous night. Torg and Krom were there too, talking animatedly to each other with obvious enthusiasm.

"That was a brilliant stroke by Ardyl to include Krom and Torg and make them leaders," whispered Barff to Rork. "Don't I just know it," said Rork, equally enthusiastically, and proceeded to tell Barff all that he had seen that day.

A loud tapping interrupted them as Ardyl struck the window with his beak.

"Thank you all for coming," said Ardyl, "I trust you have all had a most interesting day in the company of Torg and Krom," he added with a glint of amusement in his eye. "I'm sure we all thought we could fly before meeting them!" He paused while a ripple of dry laughter ran around those at the meeting. "On a more serious note, I'm sorry to have to tell you that the men with guns were down at the quarry this morning. Our observers watched them from a distance and they made no attempt to use their guns on the crows and magpies that were feeding there. Once or twice our brave observers flew closer to the feeding ground, and when they did, the men raised their guns and pointed at them. When the men had gone, we asked the other birds that were there whether they had ever been shot at, and although one or two of them had, it had not been when they were in the quarry. Unfortunately this backs the theory advanced by Rork at last night's meeting. It does appear that they are specifically targeting us gulls and therefore tomorrow's operation is still on." The passing of this information transformed the mood at the briefing, as Ardyl knew it would. "Now, without further ado I am going to hand the proceedings over to my colleague who some of you know as Wingco. Those of you who have not met him will soon find out why he has been given this sobriquet."

Ardyl stood back and a gull unknown to Rork took centre stage. He was stocky and rather square but carried himself very erect, giving the effect of being tall. His wings were folded tightly behind him and he spoke with his beak high in the air while staring somewhere into the distance.

"Right chaps. This is it! We have given the operation the code name Dirty Bomb!" This produced an excited murmur from the assembled gulls. "We are going to use one of the few weapons available to us in our armoury to hassle and chastise the people with whom we share our beautiful part of the country. We were here long before they arrived but since they settled here in all their numbers, we have done our best to live in peace alongside them. Tomorrow is our chance to show them that we are not going to be displaced and to register our strongest protest at the needless slaughter of our colleagues."

This stirring message induced a roar of approval from the audience.

"I make no claim to have any artistic talent whatsoever, but I hope that even the most uncharitable amongst you will recognise my drawing of the town and its surrounds from the air." He pointed with his wing to the dusty map and touched an area overlooking the bay. "The heavy brigade will rendezvous at 0900 hours precisely, assembling here at Potton Hill which overlooks the general target area. We will divide ourselves into two loose V formations with a similar number of gulls in each squadron. The first squadron, led by Krom, will attack targets on the beach and in the harbour. The second, led by Ardyl, will attack targets in the town. It is market day so the square will be full of stalls and visitors."

A young gull in the audience close to Rork raised his wing. "Excuse me sir, are we allowed to interrupt the briefing with questions or will you deal with them later?"

"No, I'm happy to take questions at any point," replied Wingco. "What is it you want to know?"

"At what sort of height will we be flying?" the young gull asked.

"That's a good question, young Asher," replied Wingco. "I want you to fly at around about the height of the church spire. Our attack is intended as a complete surprise and I do not expect any opposition from men with guns. However, it is better to be cautious and at that height it would be difficult for them to do any damage."

Ardyl stood up. "How are we going to judge the accuracy of the attack at that distance, Wingco?"

The Wingco paused before he replied. "I thought of that one long and hard. I don't think accuracy is over essential at this stage. The intention is to show the people of the town – holidaymakers and residents alike – that we mean business and to make them think again about attacking us. However, each squadron will have a fast, low-flying spotter who will report back to the squadron leader after each pass. Krom's squadron will have Faz as a spotter and young Jez will spot for Ardyl and his cohorts."

Rork looked around the roof and saw his young cousins. Others were looking at them too and they both squirmed with embarrassment and pride at been chosen for this important task.

"This part of the operation will cease at 1100 hours when both squadrons will land for refuelling"

"Don't you mean for reloading ammunition?" shouted one wag from the back.

"I certainly mean them both," agreed the Wingco. "Now, this is important. We are going to land back in the quarry." This last sentence brought a few low whistles of amazement from the audience. "We do not expect the men with guns to be there at that time of day," he continued, "and we will be very careful as we make our approach. However, if it is clear, we will land and hopefully there will be other humans there who will make the connection. We must endeavour to let *them* know *why*."

"When do we go in?" shouted one of the gulls under the command of Torg.

"Don't worry – your turn to take the stage comes next and I expect it to be quite a variety performance! You are all to play a ground attack role."

Again an excited ripple of conversation ran around the rooftop, especially from those who had trained with Torg. Jez suddenly realised what this meant. "But that's not fair," he hissed to Faz. "We'll miss the real fun!"

"Torg will send you off in pairs at probably ten minute intervals," continued Wingco. "You will have a more free-ranging role and will select your targets as the opportunity presents itself."

Behind Wingco, Torg stood up and stretched his wings in great curves, shaking them powerfully. "We'll get the beggars, won't we fellas?" he screamed viciously. The birds in his squadron responded in a similar fashion. Instantly the Admiral stood up and glared at Torg. Wingco knew exactly what this meant. He waited for the hubbub to die down and raised his voice sternly.

"There will be absolutely no physical contact whatsoever! I repeat, for those of you who may be short of hearing, there will be *no* physical contact. Not a nudge, not a peck nor even the brush of a feather. *Is it that understood? This is a strictly non-violent protest.*" He paused for this strong message to get home. "I'll now hand over to my colleague Ensil who will give us the weather forecast for tomorrow."

Rork knew Ensil well. They had been brought up together in almost adjoining nests and had played together and learned to fly together many years before. Rork remembered Ensil as a shy quiet bird and was surprised when he came forward to speak. Unfortunately Ensil tripped over his own feet as he approached, producing a titter from some of the assembled gulls.

"I… I… I… I'll give you the f…f… forecast for the t…t… target area from 0600 hours." he began nervously. "From a chilly start, the day will quickly w… warm up to temperatures similar to today. There will be high cloud at times although this will not be th… thick enough to obscure the sun. Visibility will be good…"

"So just the same as today then?" came a call from one of the younger ones.

"Yeah, come on Pencil – get on with it!" shouted another.

Ensil bristled with indignation and, in his anger, forgot to stutter. "There will be one important difference in the weather from today," he said, staring defiantly back at the hecklers. "There'll be a brisk onshore breeze during the morning but as temperatures rise over the land and the sea breeze fills in, this will become strong at times," he finished triumphantly. "You will need to take this into account when you take aim."

47

Cheers greeted Ensil's riposte with its implied rebuke and Wingco seized on this to end the meeting on a high note. "That brings me neatly to my conclusion. Make sure you eat and drink your fill tonight and tomorrow morning. *Do not waste ammunition* – if you are unsure of hitting the target, delay jettisoning your precious cargo until the next approach. Good hunting to you all!"

Rork half-expected the Admiral to say a few words but instead saw him turn to Wingco and nod his approval at the way the meeting had been conducted. He turned to Ardyl, "What time shall I see you in the morning, Ardyl?"

"You're not with us, old chap – special orders from on high you know."

"But Ardyl... I thought I was to be in your squadron. I volunteered last night," protested Rork.

"Sorry old son," apologised Ardyl. "More than my life's worth. If I were you I would go and see Wingco."

Rork muttered his agreement, said his goodbyes and immediately went up to the window where Wingco, the Admiral and a few others were in conversation. Without waiting to be invited, Rork interrupted them and addressed Wingco. "Excuse me sir, but Ardyl has told me that you will not allow me to fly with him tomorrow."

At this rude interruption, the gulls all turned to look at him. "Ah, you must be Rork," said Wingco politely. "I am so very pleased to meet you at last."

"Sir, I am pleased to meet you too but you must let me fly tomorrow!" replied Rork desperately.

The Admiral broke in with a gruff laugh. "Keen for some action eh Rork? Please accept my apologies. It was me who stopped you flying with Ardyl. Wingco and I want you to join our small team to help direct operations."

"But sir," cried Rork desperately "I am fully fit now and I want to fly!"

At that point Wingco stepped in. "Don't worry Rork. In

the next few days you'll get all the flying you can handle. The Admiral has spoken very highly of you and we need you with us as an integral part of our command structure. We decided to let you rest yesterday so that you could play an even fuller role in the days to come. You will be second-in-command to me so that if anything befalls me, you can take over."

Rork was completely dumbfounded by this statement. "But… why?"

"You have shown yourself to be cool under pressure and to possess sound judgment. You are already a respected leader amongst your peers."

Rork continued to mutter his protests but the Admiral brushed them aside. "Now old chap, go and get a good night's rest. This is going to be our command post for the next few days. Get yourself a good breakfast and meet us here at seven tomorrow morning."

Rork was stunned, but just in time he remembered his manners and thanked them all as he bid them good night. He walked away utterly bewildered. The events of the past 48 hours had shaken him to the core but none more so than what he had just learned. It held particular significance in light of his meeting with Turan. He desperately wanted to share his news with someone and Dew immediately came to mind. Rork deemed this remarkable, given the little time he had known her, although he thought better of trying to find her when he realised just how late it was. Anyway, he rationalised to himself, this is the wrong time for any romantic attachments to form. He was going to be giving all his attention to Operation Dirty Bomb and it may have its dangers. When he returned to his own roost he immediately fell into a deep and troubled sleep.

Chapter 7 – The Phoney War (1)

The following morning, Rork woke earlier than normal, although he didn't feel as fresh as he should following a broken night's sleep. He remembered Wingco's injunction and set off to eat a large breakfast. He was drawn towards the quarry for a number of reasons. Firstly, it was where he normally ate at some point in the day, and it had become a pleasant habit to meet with his friends and fly over the Downs to see what they could forage. Rork's great love in life was to fly at altitude and soar for hours at a time. The journey over the Downs gave him this excuse. The second reason was to gain more physical exercise in an effort to get truly fit again and the third most important reason was to test himself mentally. He justified the risk by saying to himself that it would be useful to report back to the command post if he saw the men with guns there again, but really it was to see if the landfill site held any terrors for him.

He soared quite easily over the harbour and the town, where everything seemed uncannily normal. Gulls were already wheeling over a fishing boat returning with the night's catch and others were carefully walking around the harbour perimeter, searching for any titbits dropped by the tourists the previous evening. He noticed that the gulls were either elderly or little more than half-grown chicks. He came to the foot of the Downs and found it easy to fly to the top with the help of the gentle tailwind predicted by Ensil. He flew to a vantage point that gave him a good view of the quarry and landed to consider his next move.

As he watched, several cars made their way down the unmetalled road that led to the quarry. None of the large machines were moving yet. Rork knew that it was still too early for them to start work. He decided to glide over the quarry, maintaining as much height as he could manage. With his exceptionally keen eyesight, he could see the black specks of other birds flying near or walking on the landfill site, but there were no gulls among them. As he flew, he watched another large car work its way down the approach road to the site. It drew up away from the others near to where fresh household waste had been dumped. Rork watched as three men went to the back of the vehicle and took out what he now knew were guns. He shivered as remembered the events of the other day and circled as the men took positions around the dump and made themselves as inconspicuous as possible. Rork thought that he had seen two of the men on the morning of the massacre.

He decided that nothing would be gained by going lower and turned to fly back over the Downs once more. Almost immediately he spotted a freshly ploughed field and dropped down to reconnoitre. No humans seemed to be around at that early hour, and although he still had no real appetite, he started along the furrows to seek what juicy earthworms he could find. Before too long, he was joined by other gulls that were destined to join Krom and Ardyl that day and, after making their greetings to each other, they ate in companionable silence.

It did not take Rork long to eat as much as he could manage and, after wishing his fellow breakfasters a successful Operation Dirty Bomb, he took his leave and flew back to the roof of the town hall.

Standing on the edge of the roof parapet, he was soon joined there by the Admiral, Wingco, Barff and Ardyl, Torg and Krom. He reported to them what he had seen at the quarry but surprised none of them with this intelligence.

Wingco rebuked him for going on his own, especially as others had been detailed to go there for the same purpose. They spent the next hour or so checking and refining the plans of the day, concentrating mainly on Krom and Ardyl's heavies as Torg's ground attack forces, by their very nature, were intended to be free-ranging and opportunistic.

"After you have completed each operation and before you release your chaps for refuelling, I want to have a debriefing session with them. Hopefully in this way we can learn from mistakes and use any suggestions that are offered. I would like Ensil to attend as many of these debriefings as possible and to act as our Intelligence Officer. In this way, Ensil can pass on information from one squadron to another that may be of use and he can also report his findings back to us." Wingco paused. "Have you any questions?"

When there were none, the Admiral solemnly wished Ardyl and Krom good fortune and sent them on their way to rally their troops.

On Potton Hill, Krom's 'troops' were waiting for him and chattering to each other excitedly.

"God," said one, "I hope he comes soon 'cos I'm busting for a you know what!"

"So am I," agreed his neighbour wholeheartedly. "I've eaten so much I feel like I am going to burst." There was laughter and agreement all round so when Krom eventually landed, a great cheer went up.

"Good morning all of you," Krom addressed them when the laughter died down. "I trust you have all breakfasted well this morning?"

The clamour this question brought about left Krom in no doubt that they had.

"For pity's sake Krom, please let us get on with it! It's way beyond my normal ablutions time and if we don't get airborne soon, it will be too late for me!"

This last appeal brought about such a chorus of agreement

that Krom decided an earlier start was essential. "Don't release your cargo until you are over the target area. Try and select your target and follow the path of your bomb to see where it lands. We are all on a massive learning curve and there is no doubt we will want to adjust our methods as we go along. Try not to waste your precious ammunition. Come on, let's give them hell."

Krom's cronies looked just that as they trundled over the short wiry grass of the Downs and lurched into the air. They circled the hill a couple of times while they got into formation with much cajoling and shouting from Krom. He then guided them towards the cove and the sandy beach that was their first target area.

On the roof of the town hall, Barf's keen eyes spotted them as they left Potton Hill and he alerted the others. "Damn!" said Wingco vehemently. "They've set off at least 20 minutes early. The beach will still be filling up with holidaymakers and they will waste the opportunity."

"Come on, let's go down to the harbour wall where we can watch what goes on," said the Admiral, and he swooped away across the harbour to find his favourite perch on the harbour light before anybody else got there. The others grinned at each other at their leader's keenness to observe and followed him down.

Winco's prediction was correct – the beach was far from full. Cars were just filling the last remaining spaces around the bay and people were busy unloading beach mats and parasols and cool boxes from their car boots. Krom had obviously seen this too and adapted his plans accordingly. His squadron of about 40 gulls flying in a giant square wheeled slowly around and came in from the sea towards the line of cars. Because they were busy, the tourists were blissfully unaware of what was about to occur. Only one little girl had squinted up at the gulls and pointing a finger, called out to her father.

The gulls watching on the harbour wall nodded

approvingly as they watched one small gull detach from the squadron and fly fast down towards the cars and circle them.

"Good, that's Faz," said Wingco. "It will be interesting to hear what he has to say about their accuracy."

Krom led the gulls from the front of the formation. "Steady as you go lads… Steadee… Steadeeeee… Bombs away!"

. The father of the little girl who pointed may have wished he had taken more notice of his daughter as the first of the 'missiles' squelched its way into the fabric of his new Lacoste T-shirt. He called out in disgust and looked around as a salvo of others rained down around him. In their excitement, most of the birds had released their cargo immediately on Krom's command, rather than waiting a few seconds to be over the target. Inevitably the majority missed the target area altogether and their bombs landed harmlessly on the beach. However, enough splattered around and on the line of cars for the newly disgorged occupants to realise they were being targeted. One of the most revolting results was a direct hit on a chubby two-year-old as she sat patiently in her pushchair. Her face and her previously clean sundress were covered in a bright green slime to such an extent that it caused her mother to scream.

"Hey, look what the flippin' thing has done to poor little Babe, Johnny! Get me the wet wipes quickly." Shock and the sudden attention from her mother made 'Babe' start crying raucously at the same time. "That's so disgusting. You've got to complain about this Johnny – we pay good money to come here to park for the day. We don't expect to have this sort of treatment. You've got to tell the council what's 'appened."

"What on earth do you expect the council to do about it?" replied her patient husband. "It was only a bit of bird poo – they can't stop the birds shitting you know."

A woman in a neighbouring four-by-four heard the shrieks and joined in the discussion. "Look how many birds came over and pooed at once. It's a bit weird – it looked like they were aiming at us."

"Look at that!" chimed in her husband, pointing skywards at the disappearing flock. "I've never seen birds flying in a square like that before."

"I only cleaned my flippin' car yesterday," called out the owner of the car on the other side. "Now look at it!" Like many of the other cars along the line, the roof and bonnet of his car was splattered with green and yellow/brown excrement.

After a few moments, the excitement died down and the holidaymakers continued to gather their belongings and claim their few square metres of beach for the day. A few minutes later they looked up in astonishment as the formation of gulls swept overhead and repeated the operation. Most of the missiles landed in the open spaces between the groups of visitors without causing any damage, but it was enough to start them talking about it among themselves.

Krom's birds flew back over the town towards the Downs and the quarry as arranged and were met on the way by Ardyl.

"My mob is already at the landfill site and feeding themselves fit to bust. The men with guns have gone from there now and everything seems safe enough, but just in case we have posted lookouts to alert us if they return."

Krom thanked him and they flew in company over the Downs and down to the quarry, still flying in rough formation. Ardyl's birds cheered as they all landed together. Krom gathered his birds around him to hear what he had to say. Ardyl came over to listen in too, and was quickly joined by Ensil.

"Well done all of you. I think that went fairly well for our first attempt. The problem was we went off too early, before the beach started filling up, so the number of targets was limited. Faz, what do you have to tell us about what you saw?"

Faz blushed but spoke up as clearly as he could. "All of you seemed to drop at exactly the same time so a lot of your shots were just wasted on the empty beach. The ones that did hit the cars made the people angry for a short while but only one or two were really affected. On your second pass, they were even more spread out and I didn't see any real damage being done."

"I think you're right," considered Krom. "It's alright blanket-bombing a wide target area, but if the area is smaller or narrow like that line of cars we have to learn to hold our fire fractionally from the command to ensure that we are over the target." He turned to Ardyl. "Have you anything to add to that, Ardyl?" he asked.

"No, I don't think so," replied Ardyl, "but I will try and think of a different method when I brief my own formation. I'd better go and do that now before they get constipated!"

Krom turned to his squadron. "OK chaps, stand down. Please get yourself fed and watered as soon as possible and don't stray too far away from where I can call you."

Ardyl quickly gathered his squadron around him before they had time to gossip with the others who had just landed. He explained to them what he had just learned and finished off by saying, " Krom's cronies have done extraordinarily well for a first attempt and we can learn a lot from them. However, you are 'Ardyl's aviators' and therefore much better flyers, so we are going to be even better." This brought loud cheers and whistles from the newly christened aviators and the curiosity of their colleagues from the other squadron.

"Today is market day in the town. All the stalls will be close together and there'll be lots of people – especially as we are at the height of the holiday season." He paused for effect. "Are you ready to fly?" Ardyl's aviators roared their eagerness to join the fray. "RIGHT," cried Ardyl, "Let's show Krom's cronies what a formation really looks like. Let's go!"

They took off and circled the quarry, slowly coming together in a formation altogether smarter than the other squadron. Not only was the other squadron watching on the ground, but they were joined by the men that worked at the quarry who had been curious at the unusual level of noise made by the birds. They all watched Ardyl and his flock climb over the Downs towards the town.

Ardyl proudly led his squadron down the river valley towards the town. He looked behind and saw Jez on his tail closely followed by a very neat square of carefully flying gulls. He led them over the rooftops of the housing estates, flying lower than had been agreed in order to create the maximum effect. On reaching the market square, they flew even lower over the stalls, gaining the notice of almost all of those who were present. They wheeled around the church spire, conscious of being the centre of attention, and turned once again towards the market. As Ardyl reached the other side of the square, judging that his flock were evenly spread across the market, he gave the order for them to drop their cargo of Dirty Bombs.

The effect was even more dramatic than Ardyl had imagined it would be. Many of those looking up received more of an eyeful than they had bargained for. The momentum of the bird's flight caused the projectiles to slant in under the canopies of the stalls, to land on the produce displayed.

"The beggars have done that on purpose to us," cried one of the stallholders to his neighbour. "Look what they've done to my fruit and veg!"

"Crumbs! I have never seen anything like it" agreed his neighbour. "But don't worry about your veg – at least you can wash it clean. Look what it's done to my rolls of material."

All round the market, the same sorts of conversations were taking place. The market inspector was immediately accosted by some of the stallholders.

"You see what happened? The birds did this on purpose. You've got to take it to the council and get them to do something about it."

Another trader agreed. "Not only have they damaged our stock, but if it is allowed to happen again, they will drive our customers away."

"Oh my God, here they come again."

They all looked up as Ardyl led his squadron back around the church spire and towards the market square. This time the element of surprise had gone and the stallholders were taking no chances. Most of them ran behind their displays under the cover of their canopies. Not all the shoppers were as lucky. Some were invited by the closest stallholder to take shelter too, but others were left out in the open as the second barrage from Ardyl's Aviators rained down. Although much of the birds' bomb load fell on the canvas roofs of the stalls, at least half of it fell in the aisles in between and as the aisles were so full of shoppers, many received direct hits. Still in formation, the gulls wheeled away from whence they came, leaving a chaotic market place behind them.

Most of those affected reacted furiously, disgusted by the excrement that had landed upon them. Many tried an improvised clean-up using the water of the ornamental fountain in the centre of the square. Some visitors asked the stallholders whether this happened very often, as they had never seen birds act together like that anywhere else. Before too long, the stallholders and one or two stricken holidaymakers had made up a deputation to take their complaints to the town council.

Ms Anne Rigby, the local part-time reporter for the *Western Morning News* was panic-stricken, as she had never had to deal with a story as unique as this one. She always carried her digital camera in her handbag in case the right story broke in Barlmouth. She had the presence of mind to take photographs of the damaged stalls and of the goods they displayed and was busy taking snapshots of some of the tourists before they had chance to get themselves clean when Ardyl's flock made their second pass overhead. She wildly waved the camera about, pointing it vaguely at the bird's formation and managed to aim several shots towards the birds before they left the square. The story was potentially one of the largest she had had the opportunity to cover, but she was unsure as to how to handle it. Already her mind was racing, searching for the right angle and headline. She did not want to appear eccentric, but was uncertain whether such a story would be taken seriously. Maybe the best approach was that of humour, but written humour had never been her forte.

While Ms Rigby was pondering her dilemma, unbeknown to her, another witness to the attack was already reporting the story. Local man Alex Dunwoody happened to be a very great fan of the BBC television reporter Caitlin Johnson, and avidly watched her every appearance on the local BBC news programme *Spotlight*. He phoned the BBC in Plymouth from his office above his estate agency Dunwoody and Son, which occupied a very pleasant Georgian building in the market square. Although he had immediately recognised the newsworthiness, and therefore the publicity potential, of the gulls' attack, unlike Ms Rigby he did not have the presence of mind to take photographs despite having a fine selection of digital cameras in his office to choose from. Caitlin Johnson happened to be out on an assignment at the time of his call and he was put through to the news office and a rather bored-sounding assistant. The assistant soon sounded extremely sceptical as well as bored when he heard the story from Mr Dunwoody.

Mr Dunwoody regarded himself as a very important local businessman, in his prime as an attractive (or so he thought) fifty-five year-old, and he used all his arrogance and experience to convince the young assistant that the story was a) genuine and b) extremely newsworthy. He had met Caitlin Johnson when she had visited Barlmouth some years before to open the annual sailing regatta. This had been organised by the Royal Barlmouth Yacht Club, of which he was a member, and at that time he had held the exalted position of Commodore. He used this tenuous connection freely to persuade the assistant that he was almost a personal friend. Still sceptical, the assistant wrote down the details of the story and promised to 'look into it'. In the end, Mr Dunwoody was forced to insist that the assistant phone any of his contacts in Barlmouth for corroboration of the story with an instruction to leave his telephone number for Caitlin Johnson with a request to ring him back. This must have caused enough doubt in the assistant's mind to get the required corroboration and within an hour he had telephoned Mr Dunwoody back to say that Caitlin Johnson was on her way with a camera team and would phone when she reached Barlmouth.

Chapter 8 – The Phoney War (2)

Torg's ground attack squadron was mainly composed of young and fit gulls that were chafing at the bit to see some action. They had been extremely boisterous all morning, a mood that Torg did little to discourage. He had tried to keep them in the practice area by Trevluan Point and told them to conserve their energies in readiness for the afternoon's excursions. In fact, the inactivity had affected him as badly as the worst of them and he turned a blind eye when a few of them sneaked off to watch the raids of the heavies. They had come back full of stories of the effects of the bombing, recounting in vivid detail what they considered the highlights to be.

This perceived lack of discipline had not gone unnoticed by the Admiral, whose sharp eye had picked out the unwanted onlookers. He dispatched Wingco to lay down the law to Torg and the youngsters but Wingco did not manage to dampen their enthusiasm for the task ahead. All the time he had been speaking to them, Torg had pulled faces from behind his back and had shaken his head in an all too visible disagreement of some of the things that Wingco had said.

Most of the young birds had paired up naturally with a friend or relative and Torg saw no harm in this. He paired up the remaining single birds and chose himself and one of his sons to lead the first mission. He selected the busy harbour area to reconnoitre and used his keen eyesight to search for a suitable target, while circling high above. From his vantage point he saw the white tablecloths and silver cutlery of The Waterside Restaurant glinting in the sunlight and swooped down for a closer inspection. His wingman followed tight behind. The Waterside was by far and away the most exclusive and expensive restaurant in Barlmouth, occupying as it did a prime position beside the harbour. Its continental look was no accident and a lot of money had been invested in the elegant awning that almost doubled its seating capacity in the season. Cheekily, a further six tables of four had been set right beside the harbour wall and all but one of these was occupied. Although the sun was high and hot, most of the parasols were down, making the birds' task even easier. Torg had borne a grudge against the people working at The Waterside Restaurant ever since they had intentionally left some highly peppered titbits scattered around the base of the tables after closing time. Torg had been one of the gulls to suffer a burning sensation in his throat after swallowing the tainted food. Torg selected a table occupied by two wealthy couples enjoying a holiday without the encumbrance of children. All the waiting staff at the restaurant wore black shirts covered by black aprons tied at the waist. Torg chose the moment when one of the waiters was setting down a silver tray bearing four of The Waterside's finest seafood cocktails.

The two gulls flew almost vertically down in a classic dive-bomb attack, releasing their pent-up cargo at the last possible moment before pulling out of the dive and flying to the roof of the neighbouring building to watch the reaction. One of the vividly coloured bombs actually hit one of the cocktails at full speed and the other splattered with full force on to the previously virgin white tablecloth. Both caused collateral damage by splashing the clothing of the two female customers. Both women screamed loudly. All four customers stood up in shock and looked at the mess in front of them. The two women repaired to the inside of the restaurant to clean up their summer clothes and themselves while the two men were ushered to the spare table by the embarrassed and equally surprised waiter. Torg, instantly grasping the opportunity, called to his son and swooped down to land at the mess that they had created. For a surprisingly long time, the two gulls were able to gorge themselves on some of the finest seafood available and to defecate again as they did so. Luigi, the owner and head chef of The Waterside, heard the commotion from the bowels of his kitchen and rushed outside to see what was causing it. Although he was a small man, very much overweight and about twice the age of the waiter, he had enough presence of mind to push past his employee, snatching his serving cloth as he did so. He waved the cloth furiously at the birds and shouted to shoo them away. They obligingly flew off, shrieking derisive calls as they did so.

Similar mayhem was caused by the next pair, who chose to attack a small queue of holidaymakers as they waited for the kiosk of the tourist information office to open after lunch. The gulls attacked their target sideways on the first run in and both discharges undershot the target by a metre or so. Enough faeces splashed up on to trousers and bare legs to cause a little damage and a lot of annoyance. The raid had taken place on the open space just in front of the town hall and had been witnessed by the Admiral, Wingco and Rork from their rooftop vantage point. Rork flew down and intercepted the two gulls before they made their second attack. Dolla, the leading gull, listened to Rork's observations and agreed with what he had to say. He called to his wingman to mount the second attack along the line of the queue and led the way down in a fast but shallower dive. The change in tactics brought stunning results. Although both gulls overshot somewhat this time and missed the two children at the end of the queue, the remainder of their very runny bomb loads spread nicely and evenly over the rest of it. Both the gulls perched arrogantly on the small roof of the kiosk and cackled so hard that their sides ached with the effort. Mrs Barker, who was on duty at the Tourist Information Office that afternoon, had also witnessed the attack on her way back from lunch. She saw how angry the attack had made the tourists and almost walked on past the kiosk as if she had nothing to do with it. However her sense of duty prevailed and she unlocked the door and pinned her name badge on her ample bosoms. She threw open the shutters and was met by a small but very vocal gathering.

The third party to observe the raid on the tourist office also saw it from the town hall, from an office just below the roof parapet occupied by the leaders of the gulls. Inside the office, the mayor was having an urgent consultation with the clerk to the council. Chairperson Ken Broadwell had reached the dizzy heights of the office of mayor after serving only four years as a councillor. He had achieved this not by any special effort or service on his part, but merely because no one else had volunteered for the job. He had promised himself to do just one year in office and then to step down from the council altogether. After working extremely hard running his own business, first as a bricklayer and then as a builder, he had bought land and done very well in the property boom years of the eighties and nineties. He had stood for the council, thinking he could bring his business acumen to bear, to lift Barlmouth Borough Council into the 21st century. After just six months as a councillor, he had realised that working with a committee was not for him. Being used to taking instant decisions for himself, involving many thousands of pounds, he found it hard to debate what he considered to be petty local matters of no importance. Although he was surprised to be put forward as mayor, he had decided to run for office as a fitting finale to his short public life. He had found the task easier than that of a councillor and enjoyed his minor celebrity status as he attended all the various societies and functions the small town had to offer.

Ken Broadwell was a big man in every physical way. His big round face that topped his big round body had a florid complexion. Both features were the result of an outdoor life coupled with an undimmed enthusiasm for Olde Devon real ale, consumed in quantity over the years in the lounge bar of The Bass Boat public house.

The florid face was rapidly turning puce with rage and frustration. "There, did you see that? Those newcomers are right – the gulls *are* attacking us. What do you mean we can't hold a council meeting tonight? Sod the usual three days' notice, can't we hold an extraordinary council meeting if it is an emergency?"

David Barker, the clerk to the council, was in many ways the complete antithesis of the man towering over his desk. He was small, grey, very unassuming and had retired to Barlmouth after over 30 years commuting from St Albans into the city where he had worked for all that time as the accountant to a small firm of insurance brokers. His lack of ambition there caused him to be taken for granted and his salary – and therefore his pension – had not risen like those of his contemporaries. He had taken the part-time job as Clerk to Barlmouth Borough Council to supplement his pension, not for any great feeling of altruism. The one thing that he and the mayor had in common was a wish for a quiet life and as peaceful a term in office as possible. The last thing that either of them needed was a crisis of the proportions they were now facing.

"I'm sorry Ken, we can't have a meeting. Barry Clifton has been a councillor for donkey's years and he should know better. The constitution clearly states that three days' notice must be given so even if we did have a meeting, anything we decided could be challenged for its legality."

"You and your pathetic rules and regulations. God, you local authority people are the pits! I get a phone call from the BBC asking me what is affecting the gull's behaviour round here and I don't know anything about it!" The mayor bellowed his anger. "Since then my phone hasn't stopped ringing with people complaining, threatening to sue the council and demanding some sort of action. The BBC is sending blooming cameras here, for Christ's sake – we've got to be seen to be doing something."

"Then do as I originally suggested, Ken," replied the clerk calmly. "Hold a public meeting in the council chambers to get a proper feeling from the town before we decide on any action. That way we can say that it was the feeling of the meeting that led us to take whatever course of action we decide, so if it goes wrong *we won't be to blame.*"

Ken Broadwell slumped into a chair and tried to calm himself and think this suggestion through. "I suppose you're right," he reluctantly agreed. "At least I can tell the BBC that we're doing something on the very first day of the trouble starting. Do you know of any other council that has had similar problems?"

The little man's face brightened with relief as he sensed the tirade was over. "I don't think I've ever heard of anywhere where gulls are working together to cause problems," he replied thoughtfully. "I have read that sheer numbers of gulls have caused problems and I know you have to have a special licence if you want to cull them as some of them are a protected species. I vaguely remember something about spraying the nests with oil. Let me get Marion busy preparing notices for tonight's meeting and I will see if I can look up some more information. Shall we meet about 7 before the meeting – say at 7.30 and I can brief you with anything I have found?"

Krom and his cronies had watched Ardyl's Aviators fly out of the quarry on their first mission and had watched them return from it. They had seen the neat formation and soon heard of their success in what Ardyl called 'the saturation bombing of the market place'. Krom was very conscious of the relative failure of his first foray and was desperate to show that he could do better. In a fairly black mood, he led his squadron away from the quarry, instructing them all to land at the top of Potton Hill for a briefing without unwanted ears listening in. He outlined his intentions to them and they listened in a concentrated silence that was a measure of their determination to improve too. They took off in a much neater rectangular formation without needing much coercion from Krom. They flew four abreast low over the hill and, maintaining station, used a straight dry-stone wall as an imaginary target. Of course no actual bombs were used. Faz stood on the wall to observe the 'attack' and was very proud to offer an opinion as to its success when Krom asked for it. Satisfied with his report, Krom led the squadron towards the town in search of a target.

As they flew down towards the harbour, Krom spied just what he had been hoping for. Coming out of the harbour mouth towards the open sea was the Kate Ellen, a fishing boat that belonged to Malcolm Kendall. Malcolm had long since given up on the highs and lows of catching fish for himself, as like all young family men, his high mortgage had to be paid each and every month. Not wanting to give up the sea altogether, he had converted his beloved trawler so that it could take out parties of sea anglers for the day. Most of these trippers were tourists doing it on the spur of the moment and so for them he had a selection of rods and lines that they could also hire. Today however he was taking out his favourite group of people – a party from Barlmouth Sea Anglers Club. Unlike the newcomers, the club members knew what they were doing and where they wanted to do it. By and large they didn't get seasick and were happy to turn out in nearly all weathers. Best of all, they spoke Malcolm's language of sea and fish and usually were very generous with the copious quantities of beers they took on board. Malcolm kindly assisted in this by ensuring he had spare boxes of ice to keep the bottles perfectly chilled.

Since boarding the Kate Ellen, there had only been one

topic of conversation for the group. Each person there had a tale to tell about the strange behaviour of the gulls, which some found funny and others found infuriating. In the latter camp, but slightly beyond mere infuriation, was Tom Cartwright, who owned and ran Barlmouth's only bakery. In the summer months, his habit was to rise with the sun and go to work to cope with the vastly increased workload created by the tourists. His work was finished by 10 am on a good day and by 11 on a bad. He had baked enough bread and rolls and cakes and savouries – including monstrous quantities of Cornish pasties – and by this time felt that he had earned his keep. He left it to his wife to run the bakery shop as he had very little time for people and even less time for 'bloomin' newcomers'. His wife on the other hand looked forward to the summer months when strangers came to brighten their small community, and she and her staff enjoyed the banter and the laughter. Just before leaving to go on the fishing trip, Tom had been helping his young van driver to load trays of his products into the van. According to him, they had been repeatedly attacked by two huge and very aggressive gulls that caused a vast amount of damage to his stock that was destined for outlying shops and restaurants. He had been obliged to return to the bakery and knock up several new batches to replace the damaged goods. He couldn't let people down now, could he?

Krom decided that a stern attack on the Kate Ellen had the best chance of success and he led his flock in a high and wide circle to line them up over the vessel's wake. He reasoned that the closing speed over the trawler would be reduced by a following assault and would therefore increase the odds of the missiles striking the target. He and his close family and his ancestors were true *sea*gulls, imbued with a tradition of following fishing boats. As Krom led his squadron down into the attack, he felt it was curiously appropriate to be doing so again. Every nerve ending in his body stood on end and all his senses seemed much more alive than usual. He wondered if the rest of the birds behind him felt as he did.

Krom's tactical skills did not extend yet to thinking about the sun's position but, without realising it, he was also leading his squadron into the attack with the sun directly behind them. So it was that those on the Kate Ellen were blissfully unaware as to what was about to befall them. The 'cascade' method of attack devised by Krom worked wonderfully, succeeding beyond Krom's wildest dreams. As each line of four birds came out of their shallow dive and caught up with the trawler, they released their load with unerring accuracy. Chaos ensued. Tom Cartwright was just finishing his tale of woe when he saw the first strike hit his neighbour on his head and shoulders. Tom realised instantly was happening to them and leapt towards the front of the boat where there was a canvas cuddy. The other members of the fishing party soon cottoned on when they became victims of the veritable deluge that was raining down upon them and they too sought refuge wherever they could. Most made for the tiny wheelhouse that was only designed to hold a couple of people at most. Malcolm Kendall pleaded with them to give him space, as he was barely able to steer. Others dived under the seats or joined Tom, pulling the canvas cuddy over them for the meagre protection it offered.

Unfortunately for them, the swiftness of the attack had been too great and the damage had already been done. All but Malcolm had been liberally covered with a vast amount of the droppings that had seemed to come down in one torrential downpour. Even Malcolm suffered the effects as his customers rubbed their own soiled clothing up against him.

When the fishermen realised the attack had ceased, they came out from their hiding holes and looked ruefully at each other, the boat and their equipment. Everywhere they looked was covered in an obnoxious and revolting slime and whatever they touched seemed to make matters worse. Lunch boxes and bait boxes were contaminated and even the neck end of the beer bottles sticking out from the fish boxes packed with ice were covered by the same disgusting mess. The air was blue with a dictionary – wide selection of expletives. They soon reached a consensus and decided the only course open to them was to return to the harbour and give up the excursion. As they turned through 180 degrees, they saw the second attack coming.

Although this time the group received a few seconds' warning, even more chaos ensued. In their desperation to seek shelter from the storm, individuals slid and skidded across the treacherous decks, colliding with each other and cursing each other as they did so. And thus another coat of slime was applied. As one of them remarked afterwards, the words 'adding insult to injury' did not begin to describe it. As if matters could not get any worse for the party, suddenly they did.

On their return to the harbour, the men in the Kate Ellen were busy using the trawler's bilge pumps to hose themselves and their equipment down. From the height of the harbour wall, the whole sorry business was filmed by a BBC camera crew who, although not realising it at the time, had caught on camera the opening scene of a drama the whole world was destined to see.

Chapter 9 – Breaking News

At 6 o'clock that evening, most of Barlmouth's population, residents and visitors alike, were eating or preparing their evening meal but, unusually for some, were also gathered around their TV sets. DVD and video recorders were prepared and ready to go. Very few people in the small town had been unaffected by the day's events and those who had escaped lightly certainly knew from others what they had missed. Word had quickly spread that a BBC crew was at the harbour and many had gone down to see them filming. Alex Dunwoody was better prepared at 6 o'clock than most. He had closed his estate agency half – an – hour earlier than usual, giving his staff the excuse that the day's events in the Square had left it bereft of shoppers. This was certainly true, as the market traders and council workers had spent the remainder of the day cleaning and dismantling their stalls, checking stock and discarding damaged items, as well as cleaning up the usual litter and the very unusual quantity of bird droppings. However, the real reason Alex closed the premises was to be home in plenty of time to see himself on television. He had been annoyed to learn from Caitlin Johnson that she and her crew had already parked themselves (illegally) on the harbour wall and, worst of all, had already begun filming. He had been invited to go there to be interviewed and, in expectation, had prepared his appearance accordingly. He had spent over an hour carefully brushing his even white teeth and combing his wavy steel-grey hair before donning a crisp white shirt and carefully choosing a brightly coloured silk tie that would not overshadow his film star tan. Caitlin had been polite enough to pretend to recognise him from their previous meeting and had chosen to interview him at the same time as the market inspector, to get their take on the attack they had witnessed by the massed seagulls. The interview had lasted 20 minutes or more.

Alex switched on his 42-inch plasma screen TV and settled back in his favourite armchair in eager anticipation, a large glass of chilled Chablis in his hand.

The main bulletin of the news concerned yet another political row which threatened to unseat the Prime Minister. This held absolutely no interest for Alex, as he had long since given up on politics. He considered that each party was as bad as each other and that anyway, he thought, the country was ruled by Whitehall Mandarins and World Economics, and this left no scope for the government to fulfil party election promises. The following few items concerned the continuing bloodshed in the Middle East and the intractable problems that bedevilled the area. News of a couple of juicy murders followed, linked to the outcome of a trial of an alleged rapist. After the usual sports report describing England's latest debacle in the Test series, Alex expected the weather forecast but instead, Huw Edwards introduced a short, light – hearted item to end on.

"For those of you who haven't yet booked holidays and are thinking about going to the seaside, perhaps you should think again. Reports are coming in from around the country concerning the aggressive behaviour of the gull population. In particular, we have reports coming in from Barlmouth in the West Country where the gulls appear to be working together to deter holidaymakers from enjoying themselves. Imagine deciding to take a pleasure boat trip around the bay… maybe taking in a spot of fishing, some lunch and a glass or two. Very pleasant, but imagine again being mobbed by a flock of about 50 seagulls who completely cover you with bird droppings when you've hardly been at sea for 15 minutes. Well, that's what happened to a fishing party on board a converted trawler called the *Kate Ellen* when it left Barlmouth harbour early this afternoon. Just look at the state of these poor men who suffered the attack – and when you watch the film, please bear in mind they had already spent to a lot of time trying to clean themselves up before they got back to their mooring!"

There followed just a few seconds of film that, through a slightly shaking telephoto lens, clearly showed a flock of gulls diving in formation and attacking the small trawler. The film then switched to the *Kate Ellen* as she came back through the harbour entrance and tied up alongside the harbour wall. It graphically showed the men desperately trying to clean themselves up, and the boat and its cargo covered liberally in gull excrement.

"Apparently this was not an isolated incident. The birds also mounted a massed raid on the market place where the weekly market was in full swing, and they also ran amok in pairs, dive bombing shops and people going about their normal daily business." Huw Edwards finished with a smile. "There will be more about this story in your local news that follows in a moment and a full report on *News At Ten*. Don't say you haven't been warned! Good night."

For just a few milliseconds, Alex sat there in stunned silence, and then he roared. "God, Ellen – did you see that? They are taking the mickey. They are taking the mickey! Did you see it?" He rushed into the kitchen, where his wife was busy preparing the evening meal. His wife looked at him mildly. "They're treating the whole bloody thing as a joke," he complained vociferously. "For Christ's sake, can't they see how dangerous this thing could become, let alone how expensive it's going to be if it continues?"

"Alex, calm down dear. You won't do your blood pressure any good, shouting like that. Why don't you wait and see what

Caitlin has to say on the local news before you get too carried away?"

"She obviously doesn't know what happened after she finished filming and they left to go up the coast to cover another story about some wretched boat restoration. Christ, what a cock-up! I'd better go and phone the news room again."

Alex wasn't the only person in Barlmouth to react in this way. The light-hearted treatment of this event had angered all those who had been on the wrong side of the gull's action. The only person that could have gained any slight satisfaction from the brief report was Anne Rigby, but she would be too busy to see it.

Anne had spent the early afternoon at the market place interviewing the traders and visitors, and then taking their photographs to be matched to their quotes. She was pleased that she had decided to take a serious slant on the day's events as the anger and frustration of the people she spoke to made it clear that they treated the gulls' behaviour extremely seriously. She went home and tapped out her story on her PC. Luckily her mother was out and she was able to do this without interruption. She phoned her managing editor to expect a story that was off-the-wall, to say the least, and then e-mailed it with the photographs for his attention. When news reached her that a BBC *Spotlight* crew was at the harbour, she took her laptop and digital camera down there and eavesdropped as best she could on the interviews that were taking place. She was contemplating that for the first time in her part-time career, her story might make lead story on the front page. When the *Kate Ellen* moored up and she took more photographs, she was convinced of it. After its passengers had cleaned themselves of layers of filth, she realised that she knew some of them and conducted her own interviews. She paid particular attention to the views of Tom Cartwright and his story of the extra hours that he had been obliged to put in at his bakery, learning again that it was the economic cost that was an underlying important part of the story. She used her mobile phone to speak with her editor again. They had never met, as he was a relatively new appointee and Anne's work since he had joined the newspaper had been relatively trivial until now. Anne detected disinterest in his tone of voice, although the words he said were polite and encouraging enough. When Anne informed him that the BBC crew were filming for *Spotlight* and when he heard the urgency in her voice, it convinced him she was on to something. The prospect of the more dramatic pictures of the *Kate Ellen* excited him.

"Anne, I'm going to send a senior reporter down to meet you this evening to help you cover the public meeting."

Anne protested vehemently. "Mr Gooch, there really is no need to send anybody else to Barlmouth. I can manage quite happily, thank you. It might be handy to have a photographer here tomorrow, if that's at all possible."

Her editor knew the feeling that was expressed in Anne's words and he tried to reassure her that it would still be her story. He deftly thanked her for her report and politely but firmly rang off before she could say anything further.

Anne's moment of euphoria had passed as quickly as it had come and she felt angry as she sat on a bench in the shelter of the harbour wall, hitting the keys of her laptop with untypical venom. How dare they send down another journalist to take over her story? It was *her story*, she was the local reporter who knew the people and knew the area better than any stranger. She had been born and brought up in Barlmouth and had never experienced anything like this before. Why were the gulls behaving like this? Over the years she had seen the gulls become more daring, walking – no, almost strutting – around the harbour walls among the pedestrians, foraging for any scraps dropped by them. She had heard stories of the occasional gull attacking a human being, but regarded them as being maverick birds that for some reason had gone off the rails. This was distinctly different. The birds were acting in concert, but why? Suddenly she realised that this was the most important question posed by the day's events. She changed the tenor of her report on the *Kate Ellen* and used the last paragraph to leave the question hanging in the air. She sent the story off to the *Western Morning News* using the wi-fi facility on her laptop for the first time and was surprised how easy it was. Pleased with herself again, and with a new resolve, she set out to determine the reason for the gulls' behaviour.

She looked at her watch and saw the time was a quarter to five. She scurried along the harbour and turned into the quaintly cobbled streets of Port Lane to get to Pacey's butcher's shop before it closed. She had been at school with Nick Pacey throughout junior and senior classes. When they were 10, they had sat next to each other in Mrs Wright's class and exchanged their first love letters. Anne remembered this only because Mrs Wright had intercepted one of them and caused mortifying embarrassment by reading it out to the rest of the class. To this day, at least one of her old school friends would remind her of this event if ever they were reminiscing. Pacey's Butchers had occupied its position on the corner of Port Lane and North Street for as long as anyone could remember. Nick had worked there since leaving school, first with his grandfather Percy Pacey and then with his father Thomas, who both died in harness. This was a tradition that Nick was determined to break as neither of them had lasted much over 60 years of age. Both had died of heart trouble that may have been genetic but was deemed by Nick's wife to be caused by an excess of red meat. She showed she cared by always serving fresh vegetables or salad with a meal, and he showed he cared by always drinking a glass or two of red wine with it. Mrs Pacey had been Nick's first and only real girlfriend from the tender age of 14 and had always been slightly jealous of Anne's earlier history with him. Nick flirted outrageously with his predominantly female customers, but Mrs P regarded this as just good salesmanship that didn't go further than the shop doorway.

Nick Pacey's abiding passion was birdwatching. Since he was a small boy, he had known his birds before his times tables and it was only reading their names in his bird spotting books that compelled him to read. He had long been a member of the RSPB and most of his holidays were centred round his interest, sometimes to the annoyance of his family. He was well known as a local twitcher. Anne had often written reports on his behalf and submitted them to the *Western Morning News* that used them if it needed to fill space. Nick was pleased to see 'his old flame' and invited her into the back of the shop for a cup of coffee while his young assistant mopped the floor prior to locking up. Anne refused the invitation, saying the sight and smell of raw meat made her stomach churn, but it was really because she knew the relentless Nick would make a pass at her. It was well known among the town gossips that his long walks over the Downs were not just for birdwatching, and that he was often accompanied by more than just a pair of binoculars. His female customers were his second abiding passion.

"Let me buy you a pint at The Victory instead," she asked, slightly coquettishly. "I need to pick your brain about the gull's behaviour around here before the public meeting tonight and it might be worth the price of a pint if it saves me a lot of time researching on the Internet."

Nick needed no second bidding and gave the shop keys to his assistant to lock up behind him. He telephoned his wife to say he may be in late for tea, delighted to have an alibi that enabled him to flirt. They discussed the gulls on the short walk to The Victory and sat on the harbour wall with their drinks to enjoy the pleasant early evening sunshine. A few tables further along the wall, Alex Dunwoody sat with a long-legged blonde girl in her mid-thirties. Luckily for Anne and Nick, they were in deep conversation and didn't look up. Anne gave Nick a knowing look.

"It's funny but although I love bird-watching, I don't really like gulls or any other sea birds. It maybe something to do with growing up with them and familiarity breeding contempt, but I don't really think so." Nick chose his words with care. "The constant noise they make annoys me and they cause quite a bit of damage to the house and the shop one way and another. You know the gull population is in decline, don't you?"

"No I didn't," said Anne, really surprised by this. "There seems be a lot more around here than there used to be."

"There are," Nick replied, sipping his pint. "And they are flourishing in the towns and cities because, along with magpies and pigeons, they find a lot of food quite easily. However, the seagulls as we used to know them, that nest in the cliffs, along the coast are in decline. Most species have a protection order on them."

"Have you any idea why the gulls around here are behaving so strangely?"

"Some gulls have always behaved strangely," snorted Nick. "There's a barmy one down at the car park that always attacks the old geezer who works there. I can't remember his name, but I reckon he did something to upset that particular gull one day and the gull has born a grudge ever since."

"So you really believe a gull can have feelings like that?" Anne asked.

"Yes of course I do and why not? Of course they can feel fear and they can certainly sense danger. They've got an acute sense of smell, wonderfully sharp eyesight and excellent hearing."

"Yes but they are the senses," argued Anne. "What I asked was whether they have feelings and emotions, a bit like we do."

"I'm absolutely convinced they do, Anne," retorted Nick vehemently. "If you believe a cat or dog can have emotions of

loyalty, happiness and sadness then I'm sure a bird can too."
Both of them sipped at their drinks reflectively.

"Have you actually watched them flying today, Nick? They
are not just flying around in a flock – they are actually flying
around in formation! And when they attack a target, it is
exactly that – *a target!* And they keep their formation while they
attack it!" Anne animatedly pressed home her argument.
"Surely that suggests they have powers of organisation, doesn't
it?"

"God knows, or at least I hope he does because I don't," said
Nick pensively. "And yes, I have seen them flying today but
obviously not as much as you have because I've been stuck in
the shop. But think about it for a moment. Birds must have
some form of intelligence. Just think about homing pigeons and
the huge distances they travel. Think about the vast distances
birds migrate – and they organise themselves into huge flocks,
don't they? Let me buy you a drink and then I must get off to
have a shower and change before the public meeting."

Anne agreed. She had to return home to see if her mother
was all right and to explain why she hadn't been around much
that day. Nick returned with their drinks and set them down.
"You know, I've just had a thought. Do you know little Lenny
Hewitt? He used to be a refuse collector but for some reason
he got a gimpy leg so they moved him to the council tip where
he is the gate man. You know, he collects your money on the
way in and tells you where to tip."

"Yes I know him," said Anne when she realised whom
Nick meant. "He fixed Mum's washing machine once, after
Dad died. He gets all the parts from machines that people
throw away. What about him? He's not quite all there, is he?"

"Oh he's alright. He may be a bit slow but he means well.
I see him sometimes when I'm out birdwatching. He probably
does a bit of poaching or something but he knows quite a lot
about wildlife. He came in the shop this afternoon… wanted
some bones for his dogs. We were all talking about the gulls

bombing the market. He muttered something about knowing why they did it. He may have said why, but I didn't hear it because I was busy serving. It may be worth having a word with him."

Anne thanked him and for a few moments they chatted about other things. The landlord came outside collecting glasses and exchanged pleasantries with them both. He moved off to clear the other tables and as he did so, suddenly two gulls dropped out of the sky and in an instant the first one had covered him in droppings. The landlord raised his hands defensively and as the second gull came in for his attack he instinctively lashed out. This gull was much slower and more tentative in his attack and was caught by a chance blow behind its head. It crashed to the ground, momentarily stunned. The furious landlord aimed a vicious kick to the gull's chest, resulting in a cloud of feathers as he made contact. The kick propelled the gull into the low harbour wall where it lay seriously wounded.

A couple of holidaymakers on the nearest table started to protest to the landlord that he had been unnecessarily violent, when all of a sudden the other gull returned for a second attack. It wisely stayed just out of reach while it released its second bomb load. The landlord yelled back at the couple and grabbed a furled umbrella from one of the tables. He held it by the material end and was just about to smash it down on the injured gull when two other gulls attacked him, to be swiftly joined by two more. The landlord smashed the umbrella down on the unfortunate injured seabird and turned to use it again on the others. He was not quick enough to avoid being pecked by two of them and he dropped the umbrella in pain and clutched at his head. The birds returned again and again to peck at him until most of the onlookers present, including Nick and Anne and – surprisingly – Alex Dunwoody, came to his rescue by waving various objects to scare the birds away.

It had all happened so quickly that Anne almost believed she had dreamt it. Seeing the landlord standing there, pouring with blood from various wounds on his head, brought her to her senses. Nick examined the landlord's head. "Some of these are quite bad, Mike. You'll need to get up to casualty pretty quickly to get cleaned up and maybe stitched. I'll get my car and take you up there myself."

He and Anne made hurried goodbyes and Anne left to file her third report of the day.

Chapter 10 – The War Cabinet

As the heat went out of the day, the Admiral called a meeting of his leaders at their 'command post' on the roof of the town hall directly above the council chambers. Barff, Ensil and Wingco had spent a lot of the day with him already, reporting back to him in detail all the events they had seen in the operations they had witnessed. Ardyl and Krom flew in, each seeming very pleased with himself, each claiming to be the leader of the finest force of gulls the world had ever seen. Rork arrived next, looking rather troubled and thoughtful. He had been flying high above the town when he had seen two gulls making an attack at the end of the harbour. He instantly knew something had gone amiss because two other pairs of gulls had homed in on the same target with scarcely a second between them. Rork lost altitude as quickly as possible but arrived too late to do anything. He saw people surrounding a man who appeared to be badly injured, judging by the amount of blood covering his head. While the group were distracted, he approached the body of the stricken seagull. To his astonishment, Dew got there at the same time. Both could see by the angle the bird was laying that it was probably dead. Dew put her head close to the gull's heart and listened for a moment.

"He's dead of course," she almost spat the words at Rork. "Torg's Raiders! I hope you're satisfied?"

"You were there at the briefing. Nothing like this was supposed to happen," appealed Rork. "They were under strict orders." But Dew did not wait to hear any more. There was a movement towards them from the group of people and Dew flew away, with Rork not far behind her. He tried to think of words to call her back but nothing suitable came to him, so miserably he turned towards the roost. The Admiral's greeting roused him from his thoughts.

"We're still waiting for Torg… I don't know why he should be late, has anyone seen anything of him?"

Rork looked at the others and when none of them made any reply, he answered reluctantly, "Yes sir, I have. There's been a little bit of trouble at the harbour and one of Torg's gulls has received injuries. I think they're probably fatal."

"If one of us has died, then it must have been more than a little bit of trouble," rebuked the Admiral sternly. "What happened?"

Just as Rork was going to reply, Torg flew over the parapet and landed beside them. He looked hot, very dishevelled and was shaking visibly.

"Perhaps Torg can answer your question better than I," said Rork, somewhat relieved.

"I can see you're distressed, Torg," said the Admiral somewhat more softly, "but if we're to try and save a life here, we need to know what happened straight away."

"There is no life to save Admiral. One of my birds is dead, kicked to death by that b…"

"Please tell us without the invective, Torg." The Admiral said this as a command.

Torg took a couple of deep breaths and he shook himself in a determined effort to collect his thoughts.

"My last pairing to go off this afternoon was Sedin and his cousin Url. Sedin has been very good in training and their first run this afternoon was quite successful, but Url had always been the slowest of them all. Damn it, it's my fault, I should have rejected him or sent him over to join Krom or Ardyl, but he pleaded with me to stay with Sedin and I let him. A lot of people were drinking at the tables on the far end of the harbour and as Sedin was going into attack, he saw the man that lives there. He has always been out to get us gulls, so Sedin led Url in to attack him. Sedin's attack was spot on and he splattered the man good and proper. The trouble was, the man was ready and waiting for Url. Url didn't pull out of his dive quick enough and the man caught him with a lucky punch…"

Torg looked wildly about him as if desperate for some support.

"This knocked Url to the ground and he may have been stunned or knocked out, I don't know which, but then the friggin' swine kicked him where he lay. I'm sorry Admiral, but I can't say this without swearing! My brother Steg saw all this happening. You may remember from the meeting; he thought we was all too soft so he refused to join us. He's been hanging around all afternoon waiting for something like this to kick off. When he saw Url get hurt, he and his mate just dived in and attacked the man as hard as they could. The man got a big stick and smashed it on Url's head and started trying to hit my brother, so we joined in too. We got him, so he was bleeding quite bad, and then a few more men joined in so we had to scarper pretty quick. I got here soon as I could after that."

Torg's eyes darted from one gull to another as he was relating the event and was very unsure how it was being received. To Torg, it seemed there was a long silence during which the other birds looked to the Admiral to make the first comment. In the event, it was Wingco who spoke first.

"Torg, do you remember at the briefing I gave strict instructions that there was to be no physical contact whatsoever with the men?"

"Yes of course I do Wingco, but this was different. They attacked us first."

"That's not strictly true, Torg. Your pair attacked them, remember?" Wingco reminded him.

"Yeah but he hit Url, didn't he sir?" This appeal was directed at the Admiral, not Wingco. "What were we supposed to do, stand back and watch? We couldn't let him get away with it, could we?"

"I'm sorry that you don't appear to realise what you have done," cut in the Admiral. "I was always afraid this would happen, but I didn't think it would do so this quickly."

"You were asked to obey orders," said Wingco, "but on the first day of the operation you have disobeyed them."

"I wouldn't so much say as I've disobeyed them," protested Torg vociferously. "I've just adapted to the circumstances and used my initiative."

"What you've done, Torg, is to change the whole emphasis of our action, which was that of purely non-violent protest. If you can't obey orders, what example does it send to the birds working under your command?"

Torg's feathers puffed out in indignation. "So what would you have done? Flown away and left your friend to die on his own?"

"Don't be so impertinent, Torg. I would have obeyed orders because I have to respect the overall plan that my leaders are trying to implement," retorted the Wingco.

"You've got to be kidding, mate. You're not running an army or an air force, you stuck up twit! Remember, we're just a colony of gulls and proud of it. If that's the way you stand by your mates, then you can shove your protest up your arse."

"That's quite enough, Torg!" The Admiral's voice was brittle. "I think you should leave us while we consider your position."

"Don't waste your time Admiral," Torg snapped back immediately. "I quit. I'll join my brother and a few others and we'll do things our way!" He turned abruptly round and flew off as fast as he could, turning briefly to yell, "You'll see!"

The other gulls turned and looked at each other in dismay. Krom looked particularly troubled. "I do have some sympathy for Torg, sir. It was a very difficult position for him to be in. What else could he do in the circumstances?"

The Admiral turned to him and saw the worried expression on his face. "Wingco was right in what he said, although," he turned again to address Wingco, "perhaps Wingco should have been a little less stuffy about it. Discipline must be maintained at all costs." He paused and spoke slowly after some deliberation. "Krom, just think what we face now stemming from this one incident. We have responded to violence with more violence and this retaliation can only mark the start of an ever-increasing spiral of confrontation and more serious violence. We have already seen that the men are capable of killing us from a distance without any risk to themselves. We have seen just two or three men with guns so far, but this will surely lead to a lot more trying to kill us."

Wingco shuffled his feet awkwardly. "I know I didn't handle Torg very well just now Admiral, and I'm truly sorry. Torg was already overheated in more ways than one and I should have let him cool down before I berated him."

"In fairness to you Wingco, I think Torg's fuse had already been lit," said Barff, in an effort to console Wingco and ameliorate the situation. "When I was with him earlier on today, trying to read the riot act to his troops, he had got them into such a high state of motivation, it was almost a frenzy."

"He always has been a bit of a hard case," agreed Krom. "But even so it would be difficult for any of us to turn and fly away from an injured friend."

"There's a second problem we have to contend with now," continued the Admiral. He was still aiming his remarks at Krom, concerned that if he didn't keep him on side he would potentially lose another valuable leader and possibly some of his gulls too. "We have a number of renegade gulls who are more interested in revenge than they are in finding a peaceful solution that will stop men killing us. To describe them as wild cards is an understatement. I dread to think what they will do, but I do feel it will escalate the situation wildly."

Rork had been watching Krom carefully while the Admiral

and the others had been speaking and he was relieved to see Krom nodding in agreement. "What are we going to do about Torg's squadron?" he asked.

Wingco glanced at the Admiral before replying. "I'd like you to go up there straightaway, Rork. They will need strong leadership now and you are the gull to give it. They will listen to you. Let them know what has happened and explain our thinking to them. Convince them that ours is the only sensible path to follow before Torg gets to them."

"I'll go and meet them now," agreed Rork. "Do I get them in a state of readiness tomorrow morning?"

The others looked at Wingco expectantly. "My suggestion is that we marshal all the birds exactly the same way as this morning in preparation to repeat the exercise. But I suggest we delay any mission for a couple of hours while our scouts seek what action the people are taking."

"That seems an eminently sensible suggestion, Wingco. Does everybody else agree?" The Admiral looked around and saw nods of agreement from all of his colleagues. "Right. Has anyone else anything to add? If not, I suggest we meet tomorrow at the town roost at the same time as this morning."

"Ex... ex... excuse me, W...W... Wingco," Ensil's stuttering was worse than ever. They all knew this meant he had something important to say, so they waited patiently for him to say it. "M...m... may I g...g... go with Rork, please?"

"Yes of course, if you think it will help," replied Wingco, having misinterpreted the question.

"T... Tor... Torg's younger brother was his wingman and he will go wherever Torg goes. I... I... should like to be Rork's wingman." Ensil squirmed with embarrassment. "That is, if he will have me."

"There is no question that I would gladly have you as my wingman Ensil. I know what a fine flyer you are. You always could give me a good workout in the air and I doubt you have lost any of the skills. But you are doing an important job here and I'm not sure Wingco would want to spare you." Rork looked at Wingco expectantly.

"You are an excellent intelligence officer, Ensil, and we have come to rely on your reports." Wingco was clearly playing for time while he thought about Ensil's request.

"Th… th… thank you sir but I w… wish to fly on operations. Surely one of the older birds could take my place?" Ensil looked beseechingly from one bird to another. Barff broke the silence.

"I am sure I could take on some of Ensil's duties, Wingco. Old Loddo has been plaguing me for something to do that would utilise his old teaching skills and I'm sure I can train him up to help if necessary."

Without looking at the Admiral for approval, Wingco smiled at Ensil. "That's settled then, Ensil. I wish you good hunting. We'll see you both in the morning."

Chapter 11 – Pre Meeting Meetings

For the past four or five years – certainly since her father had died – Anne Rigby had led a quiet ordered life. Prior to that, she had had her moments during her thirty-six years on the planet. She had done well enough at school to attend college in London for three years during which she had loved, lost, and loved again. After the last love withered and died, having barely blossomed, Anne had travelled and worked her way around the New World countries for a few years. On her return to England, she had worked happily on a fashion magazine based in the West End and, although she didn't reach any great position of responsibility, she had enjoyed the easy-going camaraderie of the office and an adequate social life. In short, she changed from a shy, rather plain and ordinary West Country girl into a smart and savvy working girl who had moments of (she thought) sophistication. A few Mr Rights came and went, as did a Mr Wrong who promised the earth during their two-year affair and then, when it came to the crunch, refused to leave his wife and children. Anne had half expected this to happen, so when the blow came, it was softened by knowing she did not have to take on the role of stepmother, the duties of whom she was concerned about as she had never met the children.

Anne had always been closest to her father. They shared the same gentle sense of humour and a love of sport, particularly lawn tennis. Both belonged to Barlmouth Lawn Tennis Club and when she was growing up, Anne had relished the moments spent there with her father because she had him all to herself. Her favourite memory was that of going to Wimbledon with him when she was twelve and watching Bjorn Borg play on Centre Court. It wasn't so much the tennis as having her father to herself for three whole days and exploring London together. When her father died, her mother had been unable to cope on her own. She had always been spoilt and cosseted by her husband and had been totally unprepared to face the world without him. Anne had tried caring for her at a distance, but in the end she bowed to the inevitable and moved back to Barlmouth. She had moved back into the old family home and into her old bedroom, telling herself it was a purely temporary measure, and had been there ever since. Her mother showed not a trace of guilt for depriving Anne of her independence and career and leaned more and more on her daughter for support.

Since Anne arrived home this evening, she had hardly spoken a word to her mother because her mother had not stopped talking herself. She had asked Anne where she had been all day, but Anne knew that this was a rhetorical question and that no reply was expected. Instead Anne was treated to the minutiae of her mother's day – from the lack of fresh salad in the supermarket, through the ailments of Mrs Robinson's granddaughter and on to the highlight of the week, the Thursday afternoon ladies' bowls match. The latter had been totally spoiled by a pair of nasty and aggressive sea gulls who persisted in dive-bombing the ladies who were playing. On hearing this, Anne put down her knife and fork and forgot her asparagus quiche and new potatoes for a moment. She listened with much more interest than she usually did to her mother's match reports. Facetiously, she asked whether the gulls attacked the visitors or home players but this went over the head of her mother, who was more concerned that her white skirt had been ruined forever.

When the meal was over and they were clearing away, the

subject changed to the evening's television programmes that included Anne's mother's favourite programme, *Judge John Deed*. Anne was just about to explain that she wouldn't be home to watch it when the telephone rang. "Saved by the bell!" she muttered as she went to answer it.

The caller was Steve Gooch; Anne's editor who decided (after watching *BBC News*) that he would help Anne cover the public meeting himself. Cautiously and politely, he asked Anne to meet him briefly before the meeting started. Anne sensed the contriteness in his voice. Rather than invite him to her home and risk him meeting her mother, Anne suggested they meet in the lounge bar of The Victory. She tried to make up for her earlier abruptness by telling him that she had not long left there and would be deemed by the bar staff to be somewhat of a lush, and he laughed and asked her to wear a red rose so he would easily recognise her. Anne put the phone down and made excuses to her mother. She hastily washed and changed into fresh clothes, put on her light make-up and set off to The Victory once more.

Steve Gooch felt pleasantly surprised as he introduced himself to Anne. He had only held the post of editor for a few months and until now they had corresponded mainly by e-mail. From their telephone conversations earlier in the day, he had prejudged her and expected to find a middle-aged man-hating divorcee dressed in a long, flowing, old-fashioned summer skirt and frumpy top. Instead what he saw was a young, fresh-faced woman wearing fashionable linen trousers coupled with a brightly coloured short-sleeved shirt that had enough buttons undone to intrigue without being revealing. She wore the minimum of make-up and her thick blonde hair was cut fashionably short.

Steve immediately apologised to Anne for barging in on what was, after all, her story. He asked her if she had seen the local news on television and when she said she had not, he gave her a quick résumé.

"They gave the story quite a lot of prominence. It wasn't the first item on but it was by far the longest. When the presenter, oh… what's his name, introduced Caitlin Johnson, he apologised if the impression given on the six o'clock news was that they were treating this story light-heartedly. Their film footage clearly showed 20 or 30 gulls attacking a fishing party on board a pleasure boat by dive-bombing them with their bird droppings. They showed the shocking state of the boat and its occupants who were covered in bird poo by the time they returned to harbour. Caitlin then went on to interview one of your local restaurateurs and a couple who had also been similarly attacked."

Steve's narration was briefly interrupted as a plate of scampi and chips was placed before him. Anne had declined the invitation to eat with him, but this had been his first opportunity to eat all day. In between mouthfuls, he questioned Anne about both incidents.

"Caitlin Johnson did pick up on the fact that the birds appeared organised and that the operation seemed planned and that they were even flying in formation. She went on to describe the attack on the market place and questioned the market superintendent and another chap who I think was a local estate agent."

"That was probably Alex Dunwoody," guessed Anne. "A bit smarmy, fancies himself as a bit of a womaniser, teeth glinting?"

"That describes him pretty well!" Steve grinned. "You sound as though you've had a bit of experience there?"

"Just a bit." Anne grinned back but didn't elaborate.

"You could see that Caitlin saw the funny side. She didn't go too much into the damage done by the gulls and costs involved, which I thought your report covered pretty well. She certainly didn't pose the question WHY at all."

"I think that's the key to the whole story." Anne's face lit up with enthusiasm. "I'm actually quite glad you have come here to help cover the meeting. I won't be able to be there when it starts. Our local bird enthusiast has given me a bit of a lead and I want to follow it up before I go to the meeting. Can you save me a chair?"

"Of course I can." Steve didn't ask Anne the whys and wherefores of the lead, a fact that didn't go unnoticed by Anne. "There is one more thing before you go. When they switched back to the studio after Caitlin's slot, they did say that further news reports were coming in where gulls had physically attacked a man, leaving him quite badly hurt. Do you know anything about it?"

"Yes I do," said Anne, more than surprised. "I thought you knew. It happened here. The man who was hurt was the publican. I was here too, meeting my twitcher, and witnessed the whole thing. I have already e-mailed the report to you ready for the morning. I didn't get any pictures though because my camera card was full." She went on to describe the incident in detail.

At 7 o'clock, David Barker, the town clerk, was sitting in his office persevering with the last bite of a chicken salad sandwich hastily purchased from Rice's the newsagent. He gave Rice's credit that the sandwich had been fresh once. His brief moment of peace was shattered as Ken Broadwell, Mayor of Barlmouth, burst through the door. David Barker immediately knew from the demeanour of his mayor and from the aroma he bought in with him that he had spent a much of the intervening period in the bar of the Bass Boat Inn.

"Well David? What have you discovered, my old beauty?" Without being asked, Ken Broadwell slumped into the visitor's chair opposite David's desk.

David threw the last of his sandwich and its packaging into his waste bin, turned and shuffled some papers on his desk. "Quite a lot, Ken. The good news is that we are not alone. A quick search on the internet shows there are a lot of councils facing problems with seagulls. Let me give you a few examples. Do you remember I said something about coating their eggs with oil? I knew I'd read it in an article somewhere. It was Aberdeen City Council. Apparently they have the world's largest population of urban seagulls and, if that wasn't bad enough, a lot of them are aggressive. They have come up with this idea of covering the eggs in paraffin, which destroys the embryos. The birds carry on sitting on the eggs and by the time they realise they are not going to hatch, the breeding season is over."

"That is no damned good to us then, is it?" snorted Kevin. "We need an immediate answer. Did you read anything about them attacking in gangs?"

"It does seem that gull attacks are not the rarity they once were." David Barker chose his words carefully. "They have been reported doing mob attacks on people, but not in the organised way I think you mean."

"Yes of course I mean that!" The mayor was becoming more aggressive again. "Have you read anything about them flying in formation, attacking in waves like blooming Heinkles and carpet-bombing like flipping B52s in Vietnam?"

"No, I think this is a first for good old Barlmouth," replied the town clerk, desperately trying to lighten the situation. "Eastbourne Borough Council has a terrific problem with rubbish being strewn about the streets by gulls that have torn open the bin bags. They are threatening to fine anybody leaving a bin bag out overnight…"

"What are the rules about culling them?"

"The trouble is the RSPB figures show that herring gull numbers are well down on ten years ago, and they are our most common gull. They are coming into the cities, presumably because it is easier for them to find food, but the country population is falling. You are allowed to cull them if they pose a threat to human health or other bird populations."

"That's it then!" ejaculated the mayor triumphantly. "I call an attack on humans a threat to human health, so we will cull the beggars. Right, I think we're expert enough now. We must know more about gulls than 90 per cent of the people who are going to be at the meeting tonight. Let's get on with it."

Chapter 12 – The Public Meeting

At the same time as the gulls leaders were holding their council of war on the roof of the town hall, directly beneath them another meeting was taking place. The council chambers were almost full to overflowing by the time the mayor and the town clerk entered. Ken Broadwell recognised quite a few people as he made his way to his chair and he stopped and spoke to a few of them on the way, shaking hands as he did so. A few steps behind him, David Barker spoke in a quiet whisper to one of the ushers. "He thinks he's on a presidential walkabout Pete, just look at him!" They took up their usual positions as if it were a council meeting. Mayor Broadwell pounded a glass on the table in front of him to get the attention of the assembled throng.

"Good evening everyone, thank you for coming out at such short notice to attend this public meeting. For those that don't know me, my name is Ken Broadwell and I am the mayor of Barlmouth. Although this is not a council meeting, I have offered to be Chairman, unless any of you would kindly volunteer." Ken Broadwell paused for just a moment to see if anyone had the temerity to do so. "The purpose of the meeting is to discuss the terrific spate of attacks by gulls in Barlmouth today and to see what, if anything, we can do about it. Judging by the amount of you who have taken the trouble to turn out on such a lovely evening, you have experienced some of these problems and perhaps have strong views about them. To give us all more background on the subject, can I please ask some of you who have experienced these attacks to describe them for us?" He paused for another moment. "It will be helpful to know what damage has been caused and at what cost."

A ripple of conversation ran around the audience that died almost to silence when a young man near the front stood up. He was a wiry young man dressed in a t-shirt and shorts, revealing a very tanned and fit body.

"My name is Matthew Royce. I run a business called South West Sails and we have been making sails in Barlmouth for over a half-a-century." He smiled as a witty neighbour remarked that he didn't look old enough. "We had two or three large sails laid out in our yard this afternoon ready for a final examination and test when we were attacked by a dozen or so gulls at once. They covered the sails with droppings in an instant and although we cleaned the mess off fairly quickly and easily, it was all unnecessary time and trouble. I have lived around here all my life and I have never seen gulls behaving like this before. It was definitely a concerted attack, certainly premeditated, and I can tell you, it was pretty accurate too." He gave a wry smile at the laughter this produced and sat down. Following his lead, a middle-aged woman with waist-length long hair and a highly patterned ankle-length dress rose to her feet.

"My name is Marjorie Jeffreys and I have a shop called New Age Design that faces the harbour. We sell women's clothing, jewellery and I suppose what you would call *objets d'art*. Customers have been coming into the shop all day complaining of being attacked by gulls. They have been covered in disgusting bird poo and have been pretty upset about it."

The mayor interrupted. "When you say attacked, do you mean they have been physically struck by the birds?"

"No, I don't think any of them were actually touched by the birds. They swooped on them and defecated on them. They did the same to two racks of clothing that we stand outside for people to browse through. They came again and again before we realised what they were doing and a lot of the clothing is very badly soiled. Most of it can probably be washed or dry-cleaned, but even so we won't be able to sell it as new so it will cause us quite a loss in value."

These first two speakers set the pattern for half a dozen others to follow with similar tales of woe. Luigi from The Waterside restaurant described the attack on his tables.

"My waiter, 'e is freeze'ed to the spot. I see 'e do nussing while 'e watch two of biggest of bloody gulls ever there was, standing on *my* table feasting on *my* seafood cocktail." Luigi's rotund body quivered excitedly while he was talking while his short arms gesticulated wildly in a successful effort to dramatise his story even further. "And all the time they poo poo poo all over my white linen tablecloth and my silver cutlery. I say get out of the way to 'im and I say get out of the way to the bloody gulls!" The laugh that this raised continued for quite a few moments which made Luigi all the more indignant.

"Is not funny! Is my business. In summer my guests enjoy to sit outside at the table and enjoy fine food, fine wine and fine sunshine. They no expect the dirty bomb. And the ladies is scared and the men is angry. They will no come back." He raised a pointed finger at the mayor. "What you do about it? If tourists no come, I get no business. Who pay my staff? Who pay my bills? Get compensation?"

Mayor Broadwell decided this was an appropriate moment to add a more sombre note to the evening. "We do know how alarming these attacks are, Luigi. They have already cost the council a lot of money to pay overtime for all the extra cleaning we have had to do in the market square and around the harbour. I don't think there's any question of compensation being offered by the council and I doubt you will find for many of you that it is an insurable risk." He looked to his side and indicated with a nod of his head. "We have David Barker, the town clerk, with us at the meeting tonight. It is a little bit early to expect him to come up with the legal situation, but I can assure you we are looking into it. My guess is that the actions of these birds will be regarded as a natural disaster or as an act of God and therefore are uninsurable." He looked towards David Barker as he said this but the town clerk cleverly avoided the opportunity to speak and merely shrugged his shoulders.

The mayor then repeated what he had learned from the town clerk about Eastbourne Borough Council and Aberdeen City Council to emphasise that some research was already going on. David Barker sat there, lost in admiration for his elected boss. *"My God, what a showman!"* He thought, *"He's actually enjoying himself!"*

The mayor continued, "The difference in our case is that we are facing a sudden and a co-ordinated onslaught by a considerable number of gulls at one time. We have had one or two attacks in the past, but nothing on this scale. Gulls are protected by the 1981 Countryside and Wildlife Act but they may be culled if they are proven to be a danger to public health." He looked across the far side of the room and nodded as a large figure rose to face him. Councillor Barry Clifton was tall and thickset and, with his large and heavy moustache, he cut an imposing figure. He accepted his cue with relish and looked around the room for a moment in expectation of silence.

"My name is Barry Clifton and I am a councillor here in Barlmouth. Mr Mayor, I think most of your speakers will already think their health has been jeopardised by the filthy action of these gulls. Most of us will have seen BBC *Spotlight* earlier this evening and the dreadful state of a fishing party that was attacked by a large flock of gulls. This morning, the marketplace was attacked by large numbers of gulls just as it was at its busiest. I have received many complaints from stallholders and customers alike that were on the receiving end of this vicious attack. The market was forced to close early to allow the stallholders and street cleaners to clean the stalls and the area up. You have already heard of many more individual attacks in the hall tonight, and there are probably many more which have gone unreported as yet. Perhaps some of you don't yet know, but Mike Frost, the landlord of The Victory Hotel, was attacked by a large number of gulls as he was collecting glasses from the outside tables of his pub. He has suffered severe lacerations to his head and face. Luckily there is no harm to his eyes, and he is having treatment in the casualty department of our hospital as we speak."

A hum of conversation zipped around the room and demonstrated that this was news to most of those present. "Mr Mayor, I think the danger to public health is proven and I would like to propose that we make an immediate and extensive cull of our gull population to prevent any repeat of today."

This suggestion brought about an immediate and noisy reaction from the assembly. There were many cries of "Hear, hear," but then there were also cries of "shame" and "totally over – the – top" to be heard.

Ken Broadwell spotted a diminutive figure standing in the centre of the room, patiently waiting to speak. He stood up to quell the clamour and when it died down somewhat, he reminded people they would all get an opportunity to put a point of view to the meeting. "Now can we let this young lady speak as she has been patiently waiting to put her point of view forward for some time."

The young lady in question was not really young at all but, like a lot of a small people, she carried her age well. She was simply dressed in denim jeans and the sort of t-shirt that a teenager would wear, but she did this easily and without a trace or suggestion of being mutton dressed as lamb. "My name is Felicity Dawson and I own an art gallery in Fore Street which is called 'Cry of the Gulls'. I am totally shocked and outraged at the suggestion of the last speaker." She paused and turned to look at Barry Clifton with such an expression of disdain and disapproval that it caused silence around the room. "Gulls are amongst the most beautiful of God's creatures and they normally enhance every day of our lives. They soar over the cliff tops and beaches so gracefully that I am staggered anyone could contemplate destroying them." Felicity Dawson's accent was as polished as cut crystal and was reminiscent of that of the Queen. Without raising her voice, she had her audience in thrall and she used this gift of public speaking to press home her point of view. "The gull population in Barlmouth was established long before the town and, God willing and without our interference, will still be here long after the town has disappeared. We are here to share our world with God's creatures, not to impose ourselves upon them. Certainly not to destroy them just because they cause us inconvenience. My own suggestion is that we do nothing until we establish beyond doubt that this new behaviour of the gulls is what we can expect of them from now on."

The last two speakers certainly polarised the views of the meeting. More speakers stood up to align themselves with either Barry Clifton or Felicity Dawson and this seemed to elect them as unofficial leaders for their point of view. Few of the new speakers had much to add and none of them spoke as eloquently. Ken Broadwell sought a way to bring the meeting to a conclusion.

"There is one person in the audience who we haven't heard from so far and he is well known in our small community as something of an expert in ornithology. I refer of course to Nick Pacey, our local butcher. I would like to hear your take on this, Nick."

Before Nick Pacey could take up his invitation a voice from the back of the hall yelled out, "Yeah, he's an expert on our local bird population all right!" This bought out much needed guffaws of laughter and caused Nick to go bright red as he stood up to speak.

"Thank you for the introduction, Mr Mayor. I think it's

overstating it somewhat to describe me as an expert, but bird-watching has been my hobby for as long as I can remember." This created more laughter that Nick good-naturedly took in his stride. "I am a member of the RSPB and I do know that they are concerned at the falling numbers of our gull population. The most common gull is the herring gull and these have halved in numbers over the last 10 years. Instead of being predominantly shore birds, the gulls have moved in to our towns and cities – presumably because they find it easy to find food. Perhaps over fishing of our seas has something to do with it. There is no doubt that gulls are causing a lot of damage and creating a lot of mess. They have been described as the new rats." People in the hall realised that Nick was speaking with a depth of knowledge and they listened intently.

"There have been a lot of stories around for years about gulls attacking humans and this normally occurs in the breeding season. It is a natural reaction for a gull to fiercely defend what it sees as an attack on its young. These attacks do seem to be coming more common and gulls have even been blamed for the death of an elderly man in Wales."

At this point, Nick Pacey paused but did not sit down. Steve Gooch took the opportunity to speak without waiting to be asked and stood up.

"My name is Steve Gooch. I am the editor of the *Western Morning News* and I'm here to support my colleague Anne Rigby who has been following these events closely all day. Her extensive reports will be published in tomorrow's paper. The one question that nobody has yet addressed is to ask, 'why have the gulls locally just started to behave in this way?' Does Mr Pacey have any suggestion to offer, and as far as he knows, do gulls behave like this anywhere else?"

Nick Pacey considered the question for the briefest of moments before replying.

"I have discussed this point with your colleague earlier today and I am afraid I do not have any answer to give. I am unaware of any other gull colony acting in this way. Our local gulls seem to want to do it in an organised way and have worked out how to do it for maximum effect. Maybe something has caused all of them to become unhinged."

Steve Gooch rose to his feet again. He looked towards the mayor. "Mr Mayor, may I ask a supplementary question?" Ken Broadwell was ever mindful of the power of the press and nodded his assent.

"Mr Pacey, as I understand it, when these flocks of gulls have finished a so-called attack, they fly over the Downs to the local land fill site to eat en masse. Have you any suggestions as to why they would do that?"

"I can only think that the land fill site is the most convenient source of food. A study has shown that a fully-grown seagull can find enough food in 40 minutes feeding at a landfill site to last it all day. That gives it the next 23 hours and 20 minutes to create as much havoc as it likes."

Felicity Dawson stood up and snapped, "Not all seagulls create havoc, Mr Pacey. Some seem to fly for sheer enjoyment." Those supporting leniency towards the gulls raised a small cheer at this.

Councillor Clifton took to his feet again. "Nick, everyone knows of your love of birds-" although this was an old joke by now, it still raised a few titters, "yet you seem to have reservations when it comes to gulls. I have proposed to the meeting that we carry out a severe cull of our local gull population. May I ask which way you will vote on this?"

"You can imagine that this is a very difficult question for me." The audience seemed to hang on Nick's every word. "I suppose the answer for me is that food for my family has priority over my hobby. And the main source of income for our community is overwhelmingly provided by the tourist industry. I know the visitors come for sand and sea and I suppose seagulls are all part of that. But if our seagulls' behaviour continues as it did today, it won't be long before tourists are deterred from visiting us altogether. Regretfully, therefore, I have to go with the motion for a cull."

Ken Broadwell sensed the mood of the meeting would be swung by this cogent argument and called for order. "Does anyone have anything to add or ask before we take a show of hands on Mr Clinton's proposal?"

Felicity Dawson shot to her feet again. "Mr Mayor, I would suggest that it would be an undemocratic vote to record. Most of the people present have been affected by the actions of the gulls today and, if nothing else, probably have revenge in the back of their minds. Therefore they will vote for the motion. People that weren't affected by the gulls aren't here to balance the debate."

"I don't see quite where your argument is going, Mrs Dawson." Ken Broadwell was keen to wrap the meeting up now. "This is a public meeting, open to anybody to attend and so obviously those with an interest did so. As I see it, that is how democracy works in this country. If there is no other business to be brought to our attention," he paused and craned his neck as he looked around the room to make it obvious he was open to further speakers, "then I would like a show of hands for all those who approve the motion for an immediate cull in our gull population. Needless to say, the cull would be carried out as humanely as possible. Will all those in favour raise their hands now."

The mayor looked around the hall and was relieved to see that the overwhelming majority of those present had a hand raised. "And those against then please." A small number of hands dotted around the room were raised but it was plain to see which way the vote had fallen.

"I declare the motion carried by an overwhelming majority of those present. This closes the meeting and I thank you all for attending. Good night."

Chapter 13 – Lenny Hewitt

Anne found Lenny Hewitt's house easily, just like one of his neighbours said she would. In fact, it was unmistakable. Lenny lived in the end house of a cul-de-sac of semi-detached houses that had been council built in the early 1950s. It occupied, by today's standards at least, a large corner plot that was largely laid to grass. Anne guessed that at some stage Lenny had purchased the house from the council as it had a more recent garage built in slightly different brick than the house itself. The front garden and the area around the garage were strewn with two old cars, motorbikes, an old petrol-driven lawn mower and a countless number of large toys. The garage door was open and Anne could see that it was almost full with similar items, including fridges and washing machines.

Anne knocked at the door and a female voice from an open sitting room window called out, "Come round the back." Anne threaded her way down a concrete side path and knocked at a wooden back door that had very little paint left on it. She stood there for a few moments, watching two young boys in the centre of a very overgrown rear garden. They were trying to repair a pedal cart that was missing a wheel. At the back of the garden, Anne could see woodland interspersed with rocks and could hear the noise of the River Barl as it crashed and gurgled its way down the hillside to the town. Anne knocked on the door again, louder this time, and attracted the boys' attention. One of them shouted, "Mum!" at the top of his voice, but didn't offer to help. Anne heard another faint shout of "Come in" from within and tentatively opened the door. She found herself in a kitchen, the like of which she had never experienced before. It was just a narrow pathway, barely wider than Anne herself, with so much bric-a-brac that Anne imagined it must have taken years to accumulate. She noticed one steel floor-to-ceiling racking unit full of Wellington boots of all colours and sizes. Shoes were everywhere, as were pots and pans and more and more toys. The voice yelled, "Come through," so Anne obeyed and entered the living room.

If Anne had expected the worst of this room, she was pleasantly surprised. A huge flatscreen television blared away in a corner, and there was an immense old-fashioned sideboard and an old but comfortable looking three-piece suite, but by and large there was very little clutter. A very large lady sat in one of the armchairs, which, judging by the reduced height of its cushions, housed its regular occupant. A newspaper weighed down by an ashtray rested on one arm of the chair and a teacup and saucer perched precariously on the other. The very large lady was knitting at great speed and looking at the television over half – rimmed glasses as she did so. A cigarette dangled from her lips and, as Anne watched, ash dropped onto the shelf of her enormous chest.

"Mrs Hewitt?" Anne asked rather unnecessarily.

"Oh, I'm sorry, dear, I thought you were my sister."

Anne apologised for barging in and introduced herself. "I was hoping to find Mr Hewitt. I need to ask his advice."

"Newspaper reporters don't come around Coomb Close too often to ask Lenny his advice. Has he done anything wrong?"

"Not at all, Mrs Hewitt. Nick Pacey of Pacey's Butchers suggested I talk to Lenny. They do a bit of birdwatching together sometimes and Nick says Lenny knows more about seagulls than he does. Have you heard what the gulls have been up to in the town today?"

Mrs Hewitt made a great effort and shifted in her chair.

"No m'dear. I've not actually been down there today. Have they been making a nuisance of themselves?"

"You could certainly say that," Anne said, not wishing to get drawn into a long explanation. "Lenny works at the council tip in the quarry and we think what goes on there has something to do with it."

"My Lenny knows all about the birds and the bees," chortled Mrs Hewitt. "He should do, he's got six kids! No, sorry dear, seriously he does know a lot about animals and the like. I don't know where he gets it from, I'm sure."

"Do you know if he will be very long, Mrs Hewitt?" Anne was anxious to get back to the meeting before it finished.

"He's gone up the Coomb with the dogs," said Mrs Hewitt, continuing with her knitting. "I don't think he's rabbitting tonight or he'd have said, so I don't suppose he'll be too long."

Anne was suddenly aware of the strong doggy aroma that pervaded the house and instantly felt her eyes begin to water and her nose begin to itch. She had been allergic to dogs from a very young age, although as a child she had always yearned to have one of her own.

"Does he get into the Coomb from your back garden, Mrs Hewitt?" Anne knew she had to leave the house quickly before the allergy took hold. She also knew she had no antihistamine tablets in her handbag and didn't want to chance an attack.

"Yes m'dear," said Mrs Hewitt, sensing the chance to get back to her favourite TV soap, "if you climb over the fence at the end of the garden, you will come to the footpath that follows the Coomb all the way up. You'll probably meet him coming down."

Anne thanked Mrs Hewitt and made her goodbyes. Mrs Hewitt didn't bother to get up but at least said she was pleased to meet Anne and that she hoped Lenny would be able to help her.

Anne returned through the kitchen and, seeing the pile

of dirty crockery heaped high on the draining board, felt relieved that Mrs Hewitt had not offered her a cup of tea. She strode past the two boys, who were still struggling with the pedal cart, and out of the back garden on to the footpath that ran beside the river. The garden fence had long since been flattened.

Although Anne's shoes were not exactly suitable for walking over rough terrain, she strode out with confidence, following the well-trodden trail that ran beside the river. Where the path threaded through woodland, it was dry underfoot because of the recent hot spell and where it broke into the open and Anne had to clamber over rocks, she found her shoes had a relatively good grip. The Coomb was a popular walk for holidaymakers and locals alike and Anne knew it well. Memories flooded back to her as she climbed. She remembered walking up there with her parents many times as a child, and being allowed to dangle her bare feet in the deliciously cold water. Smiling to herself, she also remembered many walks up there with teenage friends where they found more privacy for themselves, away from the prying eyes of the town. It was here she had first held hands with a boy and had been kissed for the very first time. She almost laughed out loud when she realised she didn't even remember his name!

Anne had been walking for some time and was warm with the exertion but there was no sign of Lenny Hewitt. She had passed one couple that were sitting by the river, self-absorbed in that delicious early stage of romance. A couple of dog-walkers passed her coming down and then one lone serious hiker complete with backpack greeted her with a hearty "Good evening," but there was still no sign of Lenny. She was just about to give up when she heard a low whistle. She climbed up a particularly steep part of the path and came to a plateau in a clearing that she remembered well. Here the river formed itself into a deep pool where some of her bolder friends had braved the chilly waters to swim. She found a man sitting on its edge with one cocker spaniel lying beside him and another rummaging with its nose in the foliage further upstream.

"Excuse me, are you Mr Hewitt?" Again the question was rather superfluous, as Anne knew who he must be.

"Who wants to know?" said Lenny suspiciously, turning round to look at Anne.

"Nick Pacey suggested I spoke with you," said Anne easily, sensing his suspicion. "Your wife said I may find you up here. I'm looking for some advice so I thought I'd walk up here and try to find you. I hope you don't mind."

"You still ain't said who you are," Lenny persisted.

Anne then explained who she was, whom she worked for and what she had seen that day. She explained that, like the BBC, she was covering the behaviour of the gulls and the damage they had caused and she was investigating the costs of it all and what was to be done about it. "But what I am most curious about, and what everybody else seems to be ignoring, is *why* are the gulls behaving like this?"

"And you think I can help you find the answer?" asked Lenny tersely.

"Nick Pacey thinks you may have a suggestion. May I sit down?"

"It's still a free country, you can sit where you like," said Lenny, with just a hint of amusement in his voice. He spoke sharply to his dog that snuffled into Anne's legs as she sat down. The other dog came up to her too and sniffed in curiosity. Anne stroked their ears and gazed into their mournful brown eyes.

"Your dogs are so beautiful, but please remind me to rinse my hands in the water after stroking them because I'm allergic to all breeds."

Lenny instantly ordered his dogs away and told them to lie down. Anne protested that it was an unnecessary step but swilled her hands in the cold water anyway. This seemed to soften Lenny a little bit and he asked, "So what did Nick Pacey say then?"

"He said you were in his shop today while everyone was talking about the peculiar behaviour of the gulls and he heard you say you knew why they were doing it. He was serving someone at the time and doesn't remember what you said after that."

Lenny didn't reply at first and just looked at Anne with a slight grin on his face.

"You don't remember me, do you?" he said eventually.

"No, I'm sorry I don't." Anne was surprised by this abrupt change of subject. "Where should I remember you from?"

"We was at school together. Same class. I just moved here when I were 10. That's why you don't remember. Only spent a few months in Mrs Wright's class. But I remember you." Lenny's eyes twinkled. "Writing love letters to Nick Pacey – at your age!"

Anne laughed and blushed at the memory. "Everyone reminds me of that. What happened to you after that?"

"Went to a different senior school to you and Nick. Didn't spend much time there, as it happens. School weren't for me. Went in one ear, out the other. Bunked off most the time. Went up the farm and worked for a few bob. Much better."

As Lenny was telling Anne this, she looked at him with some astonishment. She rarely forgot a face but couldn't recall Lenny at all. He was quite a small man (why do small men always attract big women and vice versa? Anne wondered to herself) with very dark weather-beaten skin that she noted was quite heavily lined for his age. His appearance was almost gypsy like. Had Anne guessed his age she would have put another 10 years on him.

"Is that where you got your love of animals?" she asked.

"Nah. Since I were a nipper. Always 'ad pets. Mice or rats

or guinea pigs or slowworms an' that. Make more sense than most humans, any road." Anne realised that Lenny was intensely shy.

"Why didn't you work with animals?" Anne's curiosity got the better of her.

"Weren't nothing going. Farm work don't pay much – that's always s'posing you can get a job in the first place. Anyway, nothing wrong with being a binman. It's bin good to me." Lenny laughed at his own little joke. Anne regretted asking the question as she sensed it had put Lenny on the defensive. "I done all right. Bought my own house, married, six kids. Got a racehorse!"

"You've got a racehorse?" Anne was incredulous and she sounded it.

"Well I owns half a race horse to be exact. Bought him last year. This is his first real season. Not had a win yet, but we've done all right. His name's Delta Bomber. You watch for him."

"Gosh, you have done well," said Anne, meaning it. "I don't even own my own home, and never got round to getting married so of course I have no children. Where do you keep the horse?"

"He's in a stud over near Marlborough. Don't tell anyone about him though. Don't want the world knowing about my business." Lenny sensed he had said too much.

Anne laughed. She was enjoying her conversation with Lenny and knew she would get more out of him if he were relaxed. She had given up any lingering ambition to attend the meeting.

"Don't worry Lenny, I won't say a word to anybody about anything we discuss without your express permission. It's more than my job is worth. I know you do a little bit on the side because you mended something for my mum once. Is that what all the stuff in the garage is about?"

Lenny decided to trust her and grinned. "It's more than just a few bob on the side. It pays a damn sight more than my regular wage at the tip. You just wouldn't believe what people throw away. There ain't nothing wrong with it most the time. And even if there is, even my kids can fix it."

"So where do…"

"Car-boot sales," interrupted Lenny, anticipating what Anne was going ask. "Finest thing that ever there was for recycling. The best ones are over at the Crescent Beach caravan parks. Newcomers there will buy anything. They take it back home at the end of their week; don't expect no guarantee, nothing." Lenny was in full flow now. "Lot of other people got second homes round here which they let out. They don't want to put new stuff in them, do they?"

Just then Lenny, put his fingers to his lips and pointed across the other side of the pool. Anne caught sight of a vivid flash of colour that disappeared as quickly as it came.

"A kingfisher!" she exclaimed. "That's wonderful. Is that why you're sitting here?"

"You see everything here if you sit long enough and quiet enough. Saw some deer drinking here last week. Beautiful."

Anne was grateful the subject had switched naturally back to animals. "You said in Nick's shop that you knew why the gulls were behaving so strangely. What did you say after that?"

"I didn't say nothing, 'cos no one was listening. Who'd want to listen to a daft old binman like me?" Lenny said this straight-faced, but his eyes twinkled brightly and he gave a broad wink. Anne laughed; she knew Lenny was sending her up slightly.

"Come on Lenny, give me a clue, please!"

"Revenge! Revenge, pure and simple."

"Revenge for what, Lenny? Are you going to tell me the story or do I have to wring it out of you?" Anne was getting exasperated but she said this with a smile.

"They been killing them, they 'ave. Every day for months."

"Jeez Lenny, you're infuriating! Who's been killing whom

for months? Has someone been killing the gulls? Who? Do they do it at the land fill site? Is that where you see it? What do I have to do to get you to tell me?"

Lenny knew that Anne was play-acting and laughed. "Now don't you say nothing like that. I'm a married man, I am. Look, between 7 and 8 o'clock every morning what's his face, um, Councillor Clifftop and that bloke from Riverside Car Sales, Derek Thingy and a couple of their mates comes down to the tip with their 12 bores. Old Robbo shows them where the freshest tippings are, especially ones with food scraps and Bob's your uncle."

"You mean they go there just to shoot birds while they feed?"

"Not birds. Gulls. Plenty of magpies, crows and the like but they don't shoot them. Just gulls."

"But why pick on the gulls?" Anne knew that Lenny had the whole story and was determined to bring it out of him.

"S'obvious ain't it? Gulls make a bit of a nuisance of themselves in the town, round the harbour specially. Bad for trade. And they nest on the rooftops now, more than the cliffs. Don't suit, do it?"

"But they are a protected species," said Anne in amazement.

"Don't matter to them then do it? Ain't no one gonna find out."

Anne suddenly saw daylight. "So that's why they shoot them at the landfill site. They can bury the evidence."

"Got it in one." Lenny actually grinned. "Or maybe got it in two, three or four!"

Anne smiled but anger was gradually rising inside her. "What makes you think the gulls are seeking revenge now, if this has been going on for months?"

"The other day they came down with their guns, same as usual. Waited. No gulls land. Plenty circling overhead, watching. Other birds on the ground feeding. Soon as a gull approach, they raise their guns but the gulls aren't stupid and fly off."

Anne was still puzzled. "They might have learned not to feed there any more, but how do you know these attacks the gulls are making on the town are in revenge for the shooting?"

"That's the clever bit, see? They gets themselves organised. They practise flying in formation. Who ever heard of gulls flying in formation?" Lenny was getting animated now and he tapped Anne on her knee to make his final point.

"They do their attacks in the town and round the harbour – hundreds of them. Then they all fly back here, make sure no guns around, and then they land." He could see Anne was still looking quizzical. "To show us! To show us they are doing it for revenge!"

Chapter 14 – Attrition

Barlmouth awoke from its slumbers to a day that already promised to be more hot and humid than ever. The air was still, with not even the trace of a breeze stirring. A big, broad grin spread across 'Cracker' Simmon's suntanned and weather-beaten face as he remembered one of his favourite DVDs that he had watched the previous evening. What particularly delighted him this time was watching it with his twin sons, listening to them laughing and sharing the same sense of humour with them. He was so absorbed in the recollection that he almost overshot the bakery. He slowed the milk float more sharply than normal, causing the bottles to jangle noisily. He jumped out and grabbed a crate of full and a crate of semi-skimmed milk from the float and turned towards the bakery.

The first beak to hit him impacted with such force on the back of his head that Cracker was momentarily stunned. If anything, his grip on the crates tightened. A split second later, the second beak struck him on his forehead with almost equal violence and his brain registered that he was being attacked. At the same time as the third beak struck his shoulder blade, he dropped the two crates with an ear-splitting crash. Blood was already running into his eyes by the time the fourth beak struck his head again, and by the fifth, his arms were raised and his hands were together in an effort to shield his head. The pain was excruciating and may have stopped his reasoning for a moment. Instead of seeking shelter in the bakery doorway or running to the side door that was always open at this hour, he crouched and then knelt with his head between his legs, his arms behind his head. He was aware of many more painful stabbings on his back and buttocks before he heard the welcome sounds of rescue.

"Get out of here you vermin, get out! Go on, shift. Get out. Out!" Cracker heard the deep voice of Tom Cartwright booming and the younger voice of Tom's driver screaming too, but his words were not discernible. He heard Tom Cartwright say "Oh, shit!" and felt arms under his body trying to pull him up. "Come on Cracker, let's get you inside."

From the roof of the town hall, the gulls' leaders heard the commotion and flew to the other side of the roof to see what was happening. They arrived as Cracker was assuming the kneeling position and saw six or seven gulls queuing up to attack his back. They watched as two men ran from the bakery, brandishing wooden implements to scare the birds off. One of the birds was easily recognised as Torg, who seemed to stare at them defiantly as he flew to safety.

"Good God!" said Barff. "Torg hasn't wasted any time, has he?"

"Let's get back out of sight where we can talk in peace," ordered the Admiral. When the birds had gathered by the council chamber skylight, he continued; "The repercussions of this are going to be enormous. This is worse than I feared last night."

"We have got to stop Torg doing this again." Ardyl's voice was tight, showing the tension he felt. "Now he's just asking for more trouble and he is bound to get it. The men will be back with their guns for sure."

"And they won't be able to differentiate between gulls, so any of us are liable to get blasted by them!" Krom could not help stomping up and down as he said this, he was so angry.

"I could kick myself for not handling Torg properly. I've

caused this problem, so it's up to me to put it right." Wingco was wretched. "I'll find Torg and his cohorts and warn them off."

"With respect Wingco, you are the last person Torg will listen to. You don't really talk his language. I do," uttered Krom grimly, and he looked up at the others for their approval.

"How do you reason with someone like that?" asked Barff.

"That's exactly why it it's a job for me," said Krom strongly. "I don't think you can reason with someone like that. He has to be *told* to stop any more attacks and if he doesn't, then he has to have the consequences explained to him."

"I take it you mean 'by the consequences', that you will threaten him with violence if he continues?" Barff spoke these words quietly. "Surely the last thing we want to be doing is fighting amongst ourselves?"

"I don't think he leaves us with any alternative." Rork sensed the melancholy in the Admiral's voice. "I have led this colony for long time and have never faced such a difficult decision. I think Krom is right. Whatever we do, we must do it quickly. Krom, Ardyl and Rork – you must find Torg and his followers as soon as possible. You must tell them to abandon their aggressive and vicious behaviour that is outside the mandate given by the meeting. If he ignores the warning, he has put himself above the council and must expect to be stopped in the most robust way!"

Barff lowered his head and shook it sadly. Wingco was equally dismayed and looked appealingly at Rork for his comments. "Let's get on with it. It's a most unpleasant task, but the alternatives are too awful to conceive. We will try and find them before we brief our squadrons."

Krom asked the question that they were all considering. "What happens to our campaign now? What do we tell the fellows?"

"They already know that Torg has broken away from us. They've heard by now that one of us has died, killed by a human. All through the night there was a feeling of restlessness in the colony. There were mutterings going on, probably from Torg and his cronies trying to gain support, but every time I went to investigate, it all went quiet."

The Admiral looked at each of them in turn.

"You tell them that we're not going to let a couple of renegade gulls throw us off the course of our original plan. We stick to Operation Dirty Bomb and continue our protest until the humans learn to stop killing us. You tell them that if they see Torg and his rebels physically attacking any people, they must try to prevent the attack *at all costs!*"

Anne Rigby yawned and stretched. She flicked the switch of the kettle and busied herself preparing the tea tray. It was still early and Anne had not yet showered or put on her make-up. She had quickly slipped on a pair of skimpy shorts and a sleeveless top. With her hair spiky and unkempt, she looked half her true age. She wanted to check over the article she had e-mailed to Steve Gooch last night. Anne still felt some of the resentment – or was it disappointment? – she had felt the previous evening when she arrived back at the town hall just as the meeting was closing, only to find that her editor had already left. She lightly toasted some bread, added some butter and marmalade to the tray and took it to her mother's room. She laid the tray down on her mother's bedside table and drew the curtains. It was a ritual she had performed many times before and she did not attempt to waken her mother, knowing the effort would be wasted.

Back in her own room, she turned her radio on and changed the station to Radio Plymouth to see if they had any coverage of the events in Barlmouth. She flicked the computer screen on just as the alarm sounded on her mobile phone. She quickly strode over to turn it off and, as she did so, noticed the message icon on the small screen. She scrolled down to read the message but not before noticing that it was from Steve and that it had been sent at 21:54 hours the previous evening.

"Meeting a hoot. Ur mayor is something else! Decision made to cull birds. Knee-jerk reaction. Tried calling you but no reply. Am returning to write report. Pls call me any time before 24:00. S"

Sure enough, there was also, voicemail from Steve saying the same thing. There was obviously no mobile signal in the Coomb. Anne mentally apologised to Steve for the things she had been thinking and, with a hint of a smile on her face, turned her attention to her article. She had been disappointed to learn of the decision taken at the public meeting and had looked for Nick Pacey to see what his take on it was. Unable to find him, she had returned home and hammered out the article in a state of high emotion. Re-reading it in the cold light of day, she noticed some phrasing that she would have chosen differently, but on the whole she was satisfied that it contained what she was trying to convey. She only hoped that Steve's own article describing the public meeting fitted in with her own point of view. The local radio station carried only a very brief account of the gull attacks but did promise to bring listeners up to date with any event that occurred today. It was still too early to ring Steve in the office, so she padded to her bathroom and turned on the shower.

Ken Broadwell picked up the phone. His head was fuzzy, his eyeballs ached and he felt unbearably tired, even though he had slept for over seven hours. In short, he had a hangover. "Hello Barry, thanks for ringing back. Sorry to disturb you so early, but it's those darned gulls again. You know Cracker Simmons don't you?... Yeah, the milkman, that's right. Well, they've done him up too. At least half a dozen gulls attacked him just as he was about to deliver a couple of crates into Cartwright's bakery... Yeah, luckily Tom Cartwright heard the crash as Cracker dropped the crates and came running out to see what was going on. Him and his boy steered the beggars off, otherwise I don't know what would have happened. As it is the poor old devil is in hospital being stitched … I know, I know… They found him on the ground, crouching to protect himself, with the gulls all having a go at any part of his body that was exposed… Thing is, I think we've got to get some decent marksmen with guns into the town centre as soon as possible… Yeah… Yeah… I know, but we don't have any real choice, do we?… No, I know… I'll get hold of Inspector Collins and check it out with him… What's his Christian name?… Wilkie?…Why?… Ian, that's right… Maybe we can get some police marksmen too… Sure, yep… Make sure they've all got current gun licences… What choice have we got? It's not safe for members of the public to walk around the town while the gulls are behaving like this… The harbour seems to be the place where the gulls are making the attacks. If we can get the guys up into rooms or on roofs overlooking the harbour, any spent shot should fall harmlessly into the water… No I don't want to close the harbour off to the tourists or anybody… Of course that's the whole flipping point… We have to see what the police say about that… Surely if we tell them only to fire horizontally or up, there can't be any danger to anyone walking below, can there?… Christ, I don't know… All right. I'll speak to David Barker; he'll get hold of the environmental health officer or Defra. I'll try and get him to get someone to issue a licence pdq… Look if you can get your boys here soon as you can, perhaps we can get the ones that are doing it early, before anyone gets the media down here poking their noses in… Sure, sure… All right, I'll see you later."

Rork circled high above the harbour, his keen eyes searching desperately for any sign of Torg and his followers. Ardyl was patrolling over the beach and its car parking area and Krom was searching over the remainder of the town centre. It was still early and the roads were relatively free of traffic, but a steady stream of cars was beginning to wind its way down the hillside. Everything looked so normal, but Rork knew that life would never be the same again for the gull colony, following Torg's moment of madness earlier that morning. Or was that really fair? Surely the madness had started with the slaughter at the landfill site? Would life ever be able to return to normal?

Rork was convinced Torg would choose the harbour, as that had been his favourite area up until now. He and Ardyl converged over the harbour wall and flew together for a few moments. Ardyl reported that the cove was fairly empty and that most gulls appeared up to be in the area of Potton Hill, feeding and preparing for the day's operations. Just as they were about to part company, Rork noticed a movement of gulls near to the building which housed the inshore lifeboat.

"Ardyl, quick! Look down there, at the end of the river. Do you see? It must be them. I'll go down. See if you can find Krom and meet me there as soon as you can."

Rork dropped like a stone to gain speed, ignoring Ardyl's shouts to be careful. He saw that it was indeed Torg and his band and he also saw what he guessed was their next potential target. A young boy, Billy Lewis, was cycling along the path by the river, blithely unaware of the drama unfolding above him. A sack of newspapers was strapped to the rack behind him and he was about to deliver the *Daily Telegraph* to Start Cottage about 50 metres away. Torg, his two brothers and three other gulls swooped towards Billy with Torg leading the way as usual. Had Billy been wearing his baseball cap backwards in his normal style, he would have seen the attack coming. As it was, he had the peak pulled down over his eyes to shield them from the early morning sun. Torg aimed himself at the patch of sun-bleached hair poking out from the back of the baseball cap. He was about to strike when he himself was struck from above on his left side with great force. Unfortunately, the

121

impact impelled him into Billy, causing him to crash his bike and land painfully on the path, where he sat clutching his bleeding elbow. The double collision knocked the breath momentarily from Torg's body and he did well to make a reasonable landing, also on the footpath. The other birds flew at Billy to continue the attack, but when Rork interposed himself between the boy and them, they withdrew and circled overhead, screeching their protest. Rork landed on the footpath, panting heavily, and turned to face Torg. The two gulls on the ground drew nearer to each other. Torg was the first to get enough breath to speak.

"I don't know what the hell you are playing at, Rork, but you are going to regret what you just did." He hissed the words and raised his wings threateningly as he did so. Showing he was not to be intimidated, Rork raised his own wings in turn and thrust his head forward until his beak was only inches away from Torg's beak. He watched Torg's eyes closely.

"You've got to stop these reckless attacks, Torg. If you don't, you're going to reap such a harvest of violence in return that the humans will wipe us out."

"What the hell gives you the right to tell us what to do? Who the hell do you think you are?" Torg drew even nearer to Rork and his eyes blazed wildly as he spoke.

"You were there at the meeting of the colony, Torg. You know what was agreed. It was a strictly non-violent plan of action, the whole purpose of which was designed to deter the humans from killing us. All you're doing is making sure they kill us more quickly." Rork was keen to talk and buy time for himself. He knew that Torg had a reputation as a good scrapper, but on a one-to-one basis he was not worried about his own ability to defend himself. Torg was small, wiry and quick but Rork was bigger, stronger, and now, nearly as fit as he had ever been. To take on Torg *and* his two brothers and their friends was altogether a different matter.

"I'd rather die fighting than live as a cringing coward like

you, Rork. When are you going to stand up and be counted?"
Torg sprang forward, using his wings for thrust, as he said this,
but Rork was too quick for him. He took off backwards, trying
to keep all six of the other birds in view.

"Try me now Torg! I am happy to be counted any time you
like. If we can't persuade you to give it up, we will force you
out."

If the other gulls needed a clear signal to join the attack,
then this was it. They swooped on Rork, using a mobbing
technique that was familiar to them all. They wheeled and
turned around Rork, seeking any opportunity to stab at him
with their beaks if they saw an unguarded part of his body.
They shrieked shrilly as they did so, egging each other on.
Rork twisted and dived, turned and flew back at them, firmly
believing that the best form of defence against numbers was
to attack. He crunched into one of the brothers – he thought
it was Steg – hearing or more likely feeling a bone snap
satisfyingly in Steg's wing. The brother dropped towards the
ground, calling out in pain as he did so.

"One down and five to go!" shrieked Rork with as much
bravado as he could muster. He was taking some hits to his
wings and body but he was giving as much as he was taking.
Torg's colleagues were also defecating with surprising accuracy
as they fought. Rork recognised this well-known tactic. It was
a ploy often used by gulls when they mobbed other birds to
scare them away from their young. Eventually, if enough
faeces stuck to the opponent, it not only weighed them down,
but also impaired their flight feathers so much that they were
forced to the ground. Rork decided to gain some height before
this happened but made sure he flew slowly enough to
encourage the other birds to follow him.

Rork made the mistake of losing sight of Torg and
suddenly felt a jarring pain in his shoulder as Torg crashed into
him. Rork spun round and had the satisfaction of feeling his
webbed feet whip up across Torg's neck, ripping feathers out

as they did so. Two other fierce jabs landed on the back of Rork's head and at the top of his leg, so he decided to fold his wings and drop. In an instant there was silence and Rork looked about him in amazement. There was a not another gull within calling distance. Below him, Rork could make out the huge figure of Krom pursuing two gulls along the riverbank and, far off to his right, he saw another bird that could only be Ardyl pursuing another one. There was no sign of Torg. Cautiously, Rork descended to the sea just off the edge of the harbour wall and with a last look around to make sure he had not been followed down, he immersed himself in the cool water and cleaned himself. Having done this as thoroughly as time would allow, he launched himself in the air – with ease this time – and turned towards Potton Hill.

Fore Street ran parallel with Port Lane and was second only to Port Lane in its importance to the town. They each ran from opposite sides of the harbour and each ended either side of the southernmost edge of the market square. While Port Lane contained the most important shops (it had once contained the smallest Woolworth store in England), such as Barlmouth's only supermarket, Barlmouth's only betting shop, and Barlmouth's only cinema, by common consent Fore Street contained the smartest shops.

At the harbour end was the Blue Water Chandlery that had been a chandlery for over 200 years. For nearly all that time it had been run by descendants of the French family, who between them had catered very well for all the marine needs of the fishing community and latterly the sailing fraternity too. When Rufus French died in harness at the grand old age of eighty-three, the French line died with him. The new owners did not care a jot for the two-hundred-year old name because they were from Enfield and therefore knew better. The new Blue Water Chandlery squeezed the thousands of items of traditional chandlery – cleats, turning blocks, brass fittings and galvanised nuts and bolts, waders and sou'westers – into a tiny maze of timber – beamed rooms accessed by a single rickety staircase. The ground floor 'showrooms' were cleared of all the old mahogany counters, the rope measuring and cutting table and the fitted display cabinets. The quarry-tiled floors were cleaned of centuries of grime, the oak beams were stripped back to the original colour of the wood and the walls were painted lemon bisque. Hundreds of halogen lights beamed from the ceiling onto shining chrome clothes racks, reflected from a dozen mirrors, and lit up the trendiest mannequins. Each clothes rack carried the latest designer label beachwear and daywear, each worth its own weight in gold. This year, yacht wear was in fashion and had its own display area in one corner of the store. Being a fashion item, it was designed for appearance rather than durability or serviceability, and was in colours no self-respecting yachtsman would be seen dead in.

If the Blue Water Chandlery was run for the benefit of its owners, then its neighbour, The Lectern bookshop, was run for the benefit of the community. Its owner, Commander Holloway, subsidised the income from his bookshop from his Admiralty pension. Sure enough, in the summer months The Lectern just about broke even, but in the winter months its income barely covered the rent and rates, let alone provided any funds for its owner. Commander Holloway carefully read most of the stock before it reached the shelves because he made sure the subject matter suited his own penchant for war biographies and anything concerning the sea and ships. It brought in a small clientele of like-minded individuals with whom Commander Holloway could yarn all day, and who would occasionally lead him to a liquid lunch at the Victory Hotel.

The next few addresses in Fore Street were private houses again, just as they had been when originally built. The advent of the two-car family brought the neighbouring large towns and cities ever-closer with their attendant hypermarkets and out-of-town shopping malls, making the smaller and more marginal shops in Barlmouth unsustainable. Some recorded their previous history on brass nameplates, showing they used to be the Old Red Lion, Compton's The Boot Makers and The Apothecary. The next brass nameplate announced Barlmouth Dental Surgery, which indeed it still was.

Shockwave was a hair salon owned by the daughter of the owners of the Blue Water Chandlery and was decorated in much the same vein. Sitting between Shockwave and Dunwoody and Son Estate Agency (which actually was in Market Square) was the art gallery belonging to Felicity Dawson that she had poetically named The Cry of the Gulls. The gallery occupied two tiny rooms, one above the other, both of which were painted white throughout, including white painted floorboards. This gave them a minimalist if not austere feel. The ground floor room exhibited five or six paintings at most, with selected pieces of ceramics displayed among them. These items were chosen carefully by Felicity herself and were by artists known to her and presumably by the art world at large. They were not inexpensive, although none carried a price tag. Visitors received a price list that carried a brief description of the painting or pottery, together with some information on the artist. Red spots marked sold items. Subject matter showed a bias toward the ocean and shoreline, although sometimes Felicity staged exhibitions on other themes too. The upper room contained far more pieces of art, still always original, many submitted by local artists and showing varying levels of talent. The prices of these were far more modest and reflected more the value put on them by the artist than the value given to them by Felicity. Price tags were on each item.

Anne opened the door of the gallery and looked about her with interest. She always enjoyed a visit to the gallery, although most of the items on the ground floor were beyond her modest means. Occasionally she had purchased some fine pieces of pottery that she cherished, but more often than not her purchases had been from the upstairs display and they became unique Christmas and birthday presents. As usual, Felicity Dawson ghosted into the room with a friendly "Good morning, Anne." Anne had always wondered whether there was a secret bell or lamp triggered by the door to alert Felicity of the presence of a potential customer, as she never failed to appear promptly.

After the usual pleasantries, Anne stated the reason for her visit. "I am covering the story of the unusual behaviour of our local gulls and I was following up a lead last night while my boss, Steve Gooch, covered the meeting at the town hall."

"Ah yes, I remember him. He asked some interesting questions during the meeting and he introduced himself to me afterwards. He seems like a very nice guy – rather attractive."

Felicity paused at this to let the last comment hang in the air. Anne felt herself blush slightly and at the same time felt a twinge of jealousy that Steve had spoken to Felicity when she wasn't there. Both feelings made her annoyed with herself. "Yes, he is new to the paper and I only met him myself for the first time yesterday. He has e-mailed me his report of the meeting and it shows you strongly standing out against a cull of the gulls."

"Of course I'm against a cull. It's really a macho men thing, isn't it? If they don't understand it, they have to lash out against it. How stupid can that be?"

Anne felt relieved that the subject had changed away from Steve and related her conversations with Nick Pacey and Lenny Hewitt. When she explained Lenny's theory of what motivated the gulls to attack in the way they had, she was pleased that Felicity took the theory on board without a hint of derision.

"If Lenny is right, that would explain everything. I can quite believe that those men took it upon themselves to reduce the seagull population without going through the proper channels to get a licence. The gulls are just defending their own kind, just like they always have done. I remember a baby gull falling from the roof above the gallery and creating a lot of fuss just outside here. Its parents came down to guard it for the rest of the day. They were so fiercely protective; they would not allow anyone near them. The noise was horrific all afternoon. The only difference is that this time they are acting collectively and they are trying to explain to us why they are doing it."

Anne was so delighted with Felicity's quick grasp of the situation that she almost hugged her. "I've just come through the square, along Port Lane and round the harbour before coming here. There have been two more attacks this morning. The first was a very serious one on a milkman outside the bakery. He's had to go to hospital for treatment. Another was on a newspaper boy near the river mouth."

Felicity interrupted her. "Oh, my goodness! If the gulls start attacking children there is no telling where this will end. It will be very difficult to stop a cull."

"Exactly my feelings, although there was something rather peculiar about this attack. I know Billy Lewis, or rather I know his mother. She's a member of the ladies' bowling team and a friend of my mother, God help her. Despite all that, she is really quite nice. I called at their house just now on the off – chance and the only thing wrong with Billy is a sore elbow where he fell off his bike when the gulls attacked him. He says that another gull prevented the attack in some way by fighting off the attacking gulls. It doesn't really make any sense, does it?"

"You mean good gulls and bad gulls? Bizarre!"

Anne grinned at Felicity. "It gets worse. Mrs Lewis won't let Billy do his paper round any more, or at least until it's safe to do so. So the gulls are interfering with the town's economy now."

"According to half of the business people at the town meeting, they've been doing that for quite a long time now anyway. Those morons seem to want to live in such a sterile world. What are we going to do?"

"That's it, Felicity," replied Anne cautiously. "*I* can't do a lot about this, except report it in the newspaper as I see it. I've just seen men with guns walking down to the harbour and I think they're going to start the cull without delay. I was hoping you could try and stop it."

"I'll do anything I can," said Felicity, "but what is there that I can really do?"

"Perhaps you could get on to the RSPB, or Natural England, and some of the other pressure groups. They must have local people that they can get down here to help us. They have probably had a similar experience somewhere else and may be able to suggest what we can do."

"What about Greenpeace? Is it their sort of thing? How about the League Against Cruel Sports? They've all got websites. I'll get on to the computer now and see if I can get some local contacts and numbers. Leave it with me, Anne. I'm on it!"

James Hawkes snuggled down on to the blanket and cradled his 2.2 rifle into his chin. "For Christ's sake, Derek, leave the bloody parasol alone. Stop fidgeting and relax."

"We're going to be up here a long time and I want to get it right. It's already far too darned hot." Derek Marsden tilted the large umbrella one more time. "There. How about that?"

"Perfect old chap, perfect," replied the plumber without even looking up. "Now for God's sake sit down, make yourself comfortable and stop acting like a bloomin' scarecrow. Have you seen Bryan's yacht?"

"Yeah," replied Derek languidly. "I was down there when she arrived and gave them a hand to warp her in. She is huge. Her mooring lines probably cost more than my little boat alone! I met Bryan's skipper. Seems like a nice bloke."

"It's not difficult to be nice when you've got a cushy job like that, is it? Talking of which, we're here to do a job too. SIT DOWN."

"All right, keep your toupee on. If it's a job, do you think we'll get remunerated for it? And will we get compensation for leaving our businesses while we save the town from rampaging herds of wild animals?"

"For heaven's sake Derek, all you think about is money, money, money and you've got stacks more of that already than most of us put together. Anyway, you haven't left your business. Your gorgeous and delectable daughter is looking after it – a damn sight better than you, I dare say." James made a rude growling sound from the back of his throat. "She could sell me the back-seat of one of your four by fours any day of the week!"

"Keep your dirty little mind away from my daughter, you grubby little manual worker, you! You're not even to think about her with your debauched mind, let alone speak about her. If I ever catch you so much as looking at her I'll stuff one of your monkey wrenches right up your backside!" Derek smiled as he said this. The two of them could go on like this all day.

"You are a two-faced so and so, Derek. Who was it had his eyes glued to the cleavage of young Clare behind the bar last night? She must be all of seventeen." He looked along the telescopic sights of his rifle and gently squeezed the trigger. "Got you!"

On the roof of the town hall, Barff fell backwards, knocked over by the force of the 2.2 bullet as it smashed into his skull. He was dead before he hit the ground.

Chapter 15 – It's the Final Countdown

"Hi, Anne. Sorry it's taken so long to get back to you but I had a meeting with the subs first thing. Jean said you sounded stressed. What's up?"

Anne was stressed but hated the thought of anyone thinking she sounded it, so she sat back from her computer and tried to relax. She had come back from her meeting with Felicity in a thunderous mood because she had still heard nothing from Steve, or anybody else at the paper for that matter. She was pounding out a report of the morning's gull attacks so far when her mobile phone rang. "My article, the one I e-mailed to you last night. Didn't you like it?"

"Hello Steve, how are you? Sorry I missed you at the meeting last night." Steve said this light-heartedly, but Anne had no time for games and deliberately took it seriously. "Whoa, whoa. Calm down Anne, I was only joking. Of course I liked your article. I think it's an amazing theory that your Mr Hewitt has put forward. I hope he's right, because it might stop that bloodthirsty lot wiping out all your local gull population."

"Exactly Steve, you've got it in one. It might interest you to know that the bloodthirsty lot as you call them have already begun the cull."

"Jeez. They didn't waste much time, did they? What the hell do they think they're up to?"

Anne explained the events of the morning to Steve and he listened in astonished silence. "I thought my article fitted in so well with your report of the meeting. I can't understand why it wasn't in this morning's paper, somewhere. Instead of that, you lead with an article on a blooming carnival in Totnes!"

"Anne, I'm sorry but it doesn't work like that. Our paper is not a true morning paper in the old tradition. Gone are the days when the editor could cry out 'Hold the front page'. Today's paper went to press at 7 o'clock last night, sandwiched between a monthly Jewish periodical and this week's *Western Property News*."

"You have to be kidding."

"No, believe me, I only wish I was."

"Gosh, I'm sorry Steve. I can't believe how naive I have been. To paraphrase you, no, I didn't know it worked like that."

"I'm sorry too but that's the way it is. Newspapers are a thing of the past. Newsprint is an anachronism, Anne. It's impossible for us to compete with the speed of the Internet, the television stations and radio. Even the national daily newspapers can't do it. That's why they are full of non time-sensitive articles and features. If they weren't, they would never get them out in time. We can print straight from your article with the technology we now have, but by the time it's on the streets it is still yesterday's news. We have the latest presses costing millions of pounds but in order to recover that investment we have to run them night and day, twenty-four/seven."

Anne wailed despairingly. "Oh Steve, but I have been so stupid. I thought my report, together with your article on the meeting last night, would be read by so many people here this morning that they would want to call off the cull. I childishly believed that I could persuade people to stop killing gulls in the hope that the gulls would stop attacking us in return."

"Don't give up hope, Anne. I'm coming over to Barlmouth in a little while and I am bringing Mickey Featherstone with me. He's our best photographer by far.

We've heard on the grapevine that some animal rights protesters have heard about last night's meeting, and are on their way to the town too. Your article will appear on the front page of tomorrow's paper, which is one reason why I was having meetings with the sub-editors. We need some good photographs to fit in the blanks and we will hold our lead article until as near to 7 o'clock as we can."

This went some way to mollifying Anne's feelings. "If we can let the barbarians know that the world is watching them, perhaps we can persuade them to call it off even at this late stage, Steve."

"You sound a little cheerier, thank goodness. Barlmouth's barbarians. Could make a good headline! Will you have lunch with me?"

Rork, Ardyl and Krom led the formation in a wide arc seaward from Potton Hill until they were approximately a mile offshore. Gradually they turned back towards the picturesque harbour town, maintaining a steady height and speed as they did so. Just about every gull they could muster had been recruited to join this grand show of strength. For show it was. Rork would never have used it as a fighting force. Young birds and old birds alike were allocated to each squadron, sorted by size rather than ability. The smaller birds from the ground attack squadron, with their numbers almost doubled by their new recruits, followed just behind the leaders. Ensil, as Rork's wingman, could have flown just behind Rork, but instead he flew proudly in the front row, delighted to be taking an active part in an operation. The two heavy brigades, similarly expanded for the occasion, followed in turn, led by Faz and Jez respectively. The more experienced birds flew on the outer edges of each group to help maintain station and there was much good-natured nagging and banter from them directed at the newcomers to ensure that not only did they keep in line, but that they also knew their place in other ways too. The experienced gulls wanted to show their recently acquired prowess.

"It's good to hear them in such high spirits," said Krom to the others. "Giving them something to do was the best thing possible. It takes their minds off the vicious schemes of Torg and his recruits."

"I'm sorry that we had to read the riot act so severely to them this morning," replied Rork, glancing backward as he did so. "We were bound to lose a few more to Torg. It's a shame, because some of the wild ones that have left us were also some of the best fliers."

"Don't worry one iota about that, Rork," protested Krom. "It was much better to find out about them during the meeting rather than have them let us down halfway through an operation. Your speech to them was absolutely brilliant. It told them like it really is and made them think long and hard about Torg's way. Instead of depressing them, you made them laugh and set them up some great challenges."

Ardyl came closer to Rork's wing tip. "I couldn't agree with Krom more and you know how I hate to say that he's right about anything! This scheme has worked out brilliantly, and if your next plan works just half as well, it will be a great afternoon. It has lifted our chaps right out of themselves and the practice session earlier on was an absolute scream!" Ardyl had been looking over his shoulder for some time. "I think we ought to slow down just a little," he said thoughtfully. "Some of the young ones are probably finding this rather tough and maybe some of the older ones too, although you'd never get them to admit it."

The formations neared the entrance to the harbour, quickly becoming the centre of attention, as they had intended. The crowds on the beach stood up to watch them go by, bathers stopped swimming and children stopped playing games as everyone looked up. The visitors strolling around the harbour paused in whatever they were doing and gazed in awe at the unusual sight above them. Those that had missed seeing the arrival of the birds became aware of the shadow they brought with them, which caused a sudden coolness to the otherwise cloudless day. Even some of the vehicles in the nearby streets came to a halt as the drivers stopped in curiosity, wanting to see what everybody was staring up at. For the few moments it took for the gulls to pass, a sort of silence fell upon the little town. Unbeknown to the birds and to the majority of the people, the whole sequence was filmed by at least two television crews, including BBC *Spotlight*. A myriad of assorted digital cameras, some in mobile phones, were pointed skyward ,to record the event for posterity and for the media. Unfortunately Mickey Featherstone and his boss were stuck in a queue of traffic some five miles away.

"Did you see that?" cried Ardyl enthusiastically.

"Wasn't it wonderful?" agreed Krom. "They were all looking at us, weren't they? That's just the effect we were after, isn't it?"

"No, I didn't mean that, Krom. I know it was brilliant and just the reaction we were hoping to achieve and all that. But did you see who that was at the harbour entrance? It was the Admiral! He was standing on the harbour light just like he always does, watching us go by."

"I saw him too," said Rork, with a more serious tone to his voice. "I think the old chap was inspecting us! He was standing there so proudly. I am sure a lot of the other birds saw him there too and they will have passed the word to each other. He was treating it like a passing out parade, but I am afraid he has put himself in terrible danger."

"Do you want me to go back and see if he is alright?" asked Krom.

"No, I'll do that. I am staying near the harbour. I do not trust Torg at all and he has been conspicuous by his absence for some time. He has some new recruits and he will want to use them. I'd almost guarantee he's watching us from somewhere, just waiting for the right opportunity to lash out. I'm going to take the front row of the fast birds to look out for Torg and his followers. In the meantime, I want you to lead the others slowly across the town again and then take them up over the Downs to the quarry. You must make sure they keep height over the town in case the men with guns are there, and you must do the same thing as you approach the quarry. If it's clear, make sure they all eat their fill before operations this afternoon." Rork flew a little higher and looked back at all the birds behind him.

"I'll go back and make sure the old bird is alright and take him somewhere safe, from where he can watch you all this afternoon." He laughed as he threw down the challenge, "I am sure you will manage just fine without me!"

Rork wheeled off, followed by Ensil and about ten gulls who Rork considered to be among the elite flyers of the colony. He led them high above the town and harbour and briefed them on the task ahead. "I want you to be vigilant at all times. You can expect Torg to make an attack anywhere and at any time, so please do not stay together all in one place. Ensil, perhaps you can give each of them a rough area to patrol. Keep within calling distance of each other and pay particular attention to the harbour area. I'll be down there with the Admiral and I will keep my eyes open too."

Ever the gentleman, Alex Dunwoody pulled back the chair from the table to allow Caitlin Johnson to sit down. Despite the heat, Alex had dressed to impress in a mid – blue linen mix suit, cream shirt and co-ordinated tie. Even his straw panama was trimmed with a blue band.

"So what was all that about, Mr Mayor?" Caitlin swatted tetchily at a fly as she spoke. The heat was getting to her. "My camera crew wait all morning for a shot of your seagulls and hardly catch sight of one, and then suddenly millions of them appear in a massive fly-past. What is going on here?"

"Our gull population seems to have gone collectively mad." Ken Broadwell felt hot under the collar and wiped sweat away from his neck. He was not so immaculate – his tie was undone and askew, his shirt collar was open and his jacket was thrown over a nearby chair. He was feeling the pressure more than the heat and thought it unfair that this problem had occurred so near to the end of his term of office. "At least they didn't attack, thank God. You do know that there have already been at least two serious attacks on people here this morning, both of which resulted in nasty injuries?"

"Does that really justify you bringing men with guns into your town-centre?" Caitlin waved the menu away as Luigi proffered it to her. "Just an Americano, please, it's far too early for me to eat." She turned her attention back to Ken Broadwell. "You do realise that I shall be asking you these sorts of questions when I interview you?"

Ken Broadwell looked at Mike Frost for some support. Mike recognised the tacit appeal for help and broke into the conversation. "You can see that I have been on the receiving end of one of these vicious gull attacks, and believe me, I do mean vicious. It was extremely painful and I am just so relieved that they did not go for my eyes on their first strike, otherwise I may have been blinded." Mike pointed at a dressing high on his cheekbone and another plaster on his forehead. "My injuries were slight in comparison with those inflicted on 'Cracker' Simmons this morning. Apparently he's in quite a bad way and they may be keeping him in hospital overnight."

"And you feel justified in the wholesale slaughter of hundreds of gulls just because of these attacks?"

"What would you prefer to see? Perhaps a child losing the sight of one eye? An old age pensioner suffering a stroke or heart attack because of the stress brought on by a gull attack?"

Ken Broadwell immediately regretted his outburst and knew it had been a mistake.

"Hold on, Mr Mayor, hold on. This is not personal, you understand. I have to ask you adversarial questions like these to bring out the arguments." Caitlin's eyes flashed a warning. "Exactly how many gunslingers *have* you got positioned around the harbour?"

"We have got ten experienced marksmen who have been instructed to only fire their weapons if they see gulls making an attack that could endanger the health of members of the public. Let me make that quite clear." Ken Broadwell regained control and said these words deliberately and icily.

"Caitlin, you saw from your own film the damage that the gulls caused by defecating on that trawler and the degrading experience that those men had to undergo." Alex Dunwoody interposed, seeing himself as a sort of wise intermediary. "And the mass raid they carried out on our market had to be seen to be believed. The gulls caused damage to stock, running into many thousands of pounds, and left the streets covered in filth and slime."

Ken Broadwell appreciated the support from his two friends and rose to the argument. "I am not taking it personally, Caitlin, so please don't worry on my behalf. Please call me Ken, by the way. We do have a problem here, and it is a problem that has to be dealt with immediately. We can't take the long-term route of interfering with the gulls' breeding programme, laying down poisons or other ways of reducing the gulls' population in the longer term. The risk of serious injury to someone and damage – costing maybe hundreds of thousands of pounds to property – however is unacceptable to the council. In this American culture of litigation, we could be sued ourselves for negligence or dereliction of duty."

They all paused to reflect a moment, while Luigi and one of his waiters brought their coffees. Luigi hovered around the table, flattered to have such important guests at his restaurant, even if it was only for coffees. Ken Broadwell felt obliged to bring him into the conversation. "You have already met Luigi and interviewed him. You've heard his comments about the effects he thinks these raids will have on his business." Luigi smiled and was about to speak but was beaten to it by Caitlin.

"Yes, yes. I know all that." Caitlin waved her hand dismissively. "But you do realise that you have some serious opposition to your idea of a cull, don't you? Just look at the banners being waved by those people at the end of the harbour wall. I've got people from the RSPB and even Greenpeace that want to be interviewed to give the other side of the story."

Barry Clifton snorted in the derisive way he always used to stifle opposition. "As usual, these protesters, or whatever you would like to call them, are highly visual but are really very few in numbers. If you go to our town hall reception desk or to the Visitors' Information Bureau on the quayside, just ask the receptionists for a look at the visitors' books and read the comments that have been left by angry visitors to our town. Tourism is our main source of revenue, and if you take it back to the source, it probably is our only true income generator. Without it this town would die. There would be no employment for young people, who would be forced away. We would just become a sterile backwater for retired people, another God's waiting room. Believe me; we have the support of most of the population, which we proved at our recent meeting."

Caitlin smiled her best disarming smile at the four men around the table. "I hope you're right gentlemen, I hope you're right. If you are, what was that cheer that went up after the birds had gone over?"

"Perhaps it was relief that the birds were not going to attack. Perhaps it was a perverse sort of irony that the great British public displays at times," surmised Barry Clifton.

"I think it was the great British public supporting the underdog, just like they always do." Caitlin brushed at imaginary crumbs on her immaculate skirt and stood up from

139

the table. The men obligingly stood up too. "You still have not answered my original question. What was the fly-past for? What did it signify? What is going on here?"

At the end of the harbour wall, the 'protesters' were asking themselves the same question. Given the extremely short notice, a surprising number of people had appeared in response to the alarm raised by Felicity Dawson. The RSPB was well represented and included the presence of Nick Pacey, who was beginning to regret his well – documented voting decision at the public meeting. Greenpeace was there in the presence of one acne-blighted teenager, although he made up for his lack of numbers by being extremely vocal. He was calling for a programme of direct action but when questioned was unable to suggest what form this action should take. He had already harangued Councillor Clifton and Mayor Broadwell and was determined to get himself on one of the television channels before the end of the day. A Natural England Land Rover was parked conspicuously and illegally on the harbour wall and the driver, who to be fair was a very recent employee, was on the phone to his employers, seeking guidance. Also on the harbour wall were vehicles belonging to the BBC *Spotlight* team and Sky TV. In spite of all this illegal parking, the police were noticeable by their absence.

Felicity had remembered some of the people who had supported her point of view at the meeting and had managed to persuade several of them to join her. Within a frenetic thirty minutes of hard work on the floor of her gallery, they had produced half a dozen or so banners that stated quite clearly which side they were on. The simplest read:

**NO
GULL
CULL**

The more expansive declared 'Barlmouth Against Blood Sports' with the lettering getting decidedly smaller towards the right hand side of the poster-sized board.

The possible reason for their presence at the end of the harbour wall gazed imperiously down on the protesters. The Admiral was well known to many of them as a local landmark and in the absence of any other gulls, he became their focus of attention. He barely moved position on the harbour light, with only the beginnings of a sea breeze stirring his feathers and revealing that he was not a statue. When the protesters were at their most vocal in leading the applause at the end of what was now becoming rapidly known as 'The Fly-Past', the Admiral remained unmoved and seemingly unperturbed. The mere act of Rork flying down to land beside him provoked a further round of applause.

The Admiral greeted Rork warmly enough, but Rork noted that he seemed strained and tired. "I do believe that was the most impressive display put on by any seabirds that I have seen anywhere in my entire life. Well done, Rork. You can certainly see what an impact it has made."

"What are you doing here, Admiral? Don't you realise how dangerous it is down here?" Rork said these words gently but urgently.

"On the contrary, my dear chap. I feel this is the safest place for me. These people seem to know me and expect me to be here as I have been for the last fifteen or twenty years. I do not feel threatened at all and I'm sure the men would not fire their guns in case they hit their own people."

Rork took a moment to look around at the people gathered nearby. "It seems I can't disagree with you. But where are the others?" he asked. "I just flew over the roost but I couldn't see any of them."

"Wingco and Loddo are visiting other gull colonies further along the coast. We thought it prudent to let them know what was happening to us in case it was happening to them too. We also may need their help here if things go badly for us in the next few days."

"I think that's a sensible idea," Rork reasoned. "I know Wingco has already had offers of help from the colony at Sheer Point. Has Barff gone with them?"

"Rork, I'm sorry to be the one to tell you, but Barff is dead." Rork could only gasp incredulously. "The men shot him as he stood at the edge of the roost looking down over the square. A powerful piece of metal, larger than the one that hit you, smashed into his head and killed him instantly. Wingco insisted on fetching your young friend Dew from the hospital, but it was obvious there was nothing she could do. My only comfort is that he would not have felt a thing."

"I don't know what to say Admiral, I'm stunned." Rork shook his head sadly. "To kill Barff, of all gulls. He was the kindest, gentlest bird I have met... Why him? I know everyone always says it but, he really did not have a bad word to say about anybody. I was so much looking forward to getting to know him better after this was all over." They both stood there in silence, comforted by the presence of each other. "I'm so sorry Admiral; I know that you and he were very close."

"He was my son," said the Admiral simply.

"Your son?" echoed Rork in amazement. "I didn't know that!"

"Not many did," replied the Admiral. He was unable to speak for a few moments because of a catch in his voice. "It seemed simpler that way. Barff was not a natural leader like you, but he did care greatly about the colony. He was not the best or fastest flyer among you, nor was he the most daring. But there are all sorts of courage and he had his own form of courage in abundance."

"I saw that," said Rork quietly, hardly daring to interrupt.

"It was his suggestion that we did not let on that we were father and son. He thought it would affect the way people thought about him and maybe hinder some of the good work

142

he was trying to do. He also thought people would see him as the natural successor to me. He knew his limitations and did not want that, even if it had been offered. My time is drawing to a close…" Rork made protestations that the Admiral waved aside. "We have to face facts Rork. I have lived a long and full life and I hope on the way, I have done some good for our community…" The Admiral again brushed aside Rork's protestations, showing some annoyance at the interruption… "There are not many gulls who reach my age and I am quite happy to meet my maker when the right time comes. There are a few of us senior citizens who have been informally discussing the question of my successor at odd times over the last few years. As you know, we have a tradition of doing this by mutual agreement rather than get involved in ugly wrangling, as they do in other colonies. God forbid, in some places birds actually fight each other for the leadership. How utterly barbaric."

Rork and the Admiral jumped suddenly as an object flew close by. One of the protesters had decided that the two gulls were in need of nourishment and was throwing the contents of a ham sandwich at them. He was standing next to a notice erected by the council that clearly stated DO NOT FEED THE GULLS in bold letters, with an explanation in less bold type underneath that feeding them created a possible nuisance and stopped gulls feeding themselves in their natural way.

The Admiral coughed as if collecting his thoughts. "You may be unaware of it, Rork, but we have been watching you for some time. You *are* a natural leader and, among those that know you, you would be a popular choice to succeed me. Not only do you lead by example, but you also have the power to think creatively, as today's demonstration has shown."

"Barff had the best brain of all of us." Rork was emphatic. "It was his idea for the dirty bomb campaign, wasn't it?"

"Yes, and it was his idea to land back on the quarry, too. He thought about that one long and hard. He spent ages discussing with Wingco and me how we were to get our message across to the people. It concerned him that one species found it so difficult to communicate with another."

"And then the other species turned around and killed him! How reasonable is that? How much thought did men put into their response to us?" Rork released some of his pent – up fury. "I'd like to get hold of the man who shot Barff and peck his eyes out piece by piece."

"Yes, but in doing so, you would be acting against all the principles that Barff believed in," came the Admiral's stinging response. "Barff was a peacemaker and hated the thought of revenge in any form."

"Then I suggest you look to another gull to succeed you as leader." Rork could not hide the bitterness in his voice. "I am not a saint. Why do you not ask Krom, or even better still, why not Ardyl?"

"Because they see *you* as their natural leader, Rork. Can't you see how you have naturally taken the role of leader in this campaign? To Krom's great credit, he has come a long way in just a few short days, but he will be the first to admit he is no great thinker or strategist. Ardyl has that ability, he is a great flyer *and* he is a popular leader among the gulls. However, he has already recognised that you have greater skills in all these areas than he, and that you are by far the most charismatic leader of your generation."

Rork struggled for the right words to frame his reply. "I think you flatter me somewhat, Admiral."

"I think in your heart you know what I say is true." The Admiral was also choosing his words carefully. "We have deliberately left you to enjoy your youth until now. The events of the last few days have thrust you into the limelight, whether you like it or not. You have succeeded in every way beyond our wildest expectations and if we come out of this desperately difficult situation with any sort of future, then you must lead the colony into a new age."

To Rork's great relief, a chunk of bread hit him on the shoulder and gave him the excuse to fly off for a few moments.

Lenny Hewitt stepped out of his small kiosk – cum-hut at the landfill site and watched the skies as the impressive formations of gulls swept overhead. His mobile phone was held to his ear as he described the scene in front of him to Anne. She had kept her promise to keep him informed and had telephoned him to say that she thought the gulls were on the way to the quarry. She told him that to see them land at the quarry would go a long way to proving his theory that the gulls were communicating their point of view. To see so many of them wheeling around and landing was enough evidence for Lenny. He whooped in delight, tears of emotion sparkling in his eyes.

Chapter 16 – 'Till Death...

Anne met Steve outside the Victory Hotel and was introduced to Mickey Featherstone. She shook a huge, very wet and very soft hand. Mickey was sweating profusely and apologised. He was a large, rather overweight and extremely bald young man dressed in tailored blue shorts and a vividly coloured Hawaiian shirt. He had carried a hefty aluminium case – presumably containing all his photographic equipment – all the way from the overflow car park at the edge of the town. They shared a round of soft drinks while Anne brought them up to date with the latest events in the town. She described 'The Fly-Past' and showed them the images she had captured on her digital camera, although the screen was too small to give anything other than a general idea of what had gone on. Steve expressed disappointment that they had missed the event but Mickey was sanguine.

"'S'alright. Don' worry 'bart it. All the rest of 'em will 'ave it. I'll look for summat different. Where d'you reckon the action's gonna 'appen?" Anne explained that most of the 'action' had taken place around the harbour so far, although there were no guarantees that it would again. "Fair 'nuff. I'll seez yuz all la'er." With that, and despite all their protestations that he should have lunch with them, Mickey slung his heavy bag over his shoulder and ambled off along the harbour wall.

"Right then, Ms Rigby. Where shall we have lunch?" Steve rubbed his hands together in expectation.

"Did you suggest to him that he didn't have lunch with

us?" asked Anne. "He doesn't seem the sort of person to turn down a spot of food."

"I didn't, and he isn't," said Steve succinctly. "If you'd have seen the amount of sandwiches he quaffed in the car on the way here, you really wouldn't be too concerned about his welfare. Now, I'm starving – where are we going?"

"I'm not sure of the etiquette in this situation. Is it really appropriate for a junior female employee to have lunch with her boss?" Anne's eyes twinkled teasingly.

Steve mimicked her. "All the best finishing schools advise in this situation that one shouldn't think of one's boss as a boss, just to think of him as a colleague who maybe wants the opportunity to get to know one better. If he does get to know one better, and likes what he finds out about one, he may be emboldened to ask one out on a proper date." Steve coloured slightly as he said this.

"But what if one's colleague turned out to be a married man? Then surely the lunch would still be highly inappropriate, wouldn't it?" The question was mirrored in Anne's face.

"I'm not married, I'm divorced and I have been single for nearly three years now." Steve dropped the banter. "I have no children, no pets and no vices other than looking after the only woman currently in my life, Sapphire."

Anne knew she shouldn't ask, but couldn't help herself. "Who is Sapphire?"

"Sapphire is a very beautiful and elegant lady who has reached a great age and has fallen on hard times. I have agreed to let her live in my garden and to spend some of my time and meagre resources helping to rehabilitate her. When I have done so, she has agreed to repay me in kind by allowing me to sail with her. When I do so, she may even let me take a friend!"

Anne laughed. "In that case, I would love to let you buy me lunch. I know just the place. Follow me." Anne led Steve around the corner to Cartwright's bakery shop. "Mine's a large Cornish pasty, please. You get them, and I'll get the 7 Up."

Having made their purchases, they made their way along the harbour wall towards the harbour entrance and, when they found a convenient space, they sat on the wall to eat their lunch. Anne patted the warm harbour wall contentedly. "If I think of all the places in the world where I would choose to eat, and if I think of all the meals I would like to eat, then I think this is my favourite spot and my favourite food."

Steve looked at Anne a little too earnestly. "Just now, I think it would be fair to describe it as my favourite spot too."

Their idyll was broken by a series of loud screams. Anne was first to react. "I think that's probably from the beach on the other side of the wall. Come on!" They shoved the remains of their lunch into a nearby waste bin and ran towards the distressing sound. To Anne's amazement, they were overtaken by Mickey Featherstone, who was moving extremely quickly for a man of his size. "It seems the game's afoot, chaps," he grinned as he ran past.

So loud were the screams and such was the desperation and urgency conveyed in them, that everyone in the vicinity moved towards their source to offer help. The first to arrive was Rork. At the first scream, he had swivelled around from his position on the harbour light and saw a commotion that was taking place at the water's edge. He was horrified when he realised just exactly what was happening. About a dozen gulls surrounded two young children who had been paddling knee high in the water and were attacking their nearly naked bodies whenever they saw the opportunity. As soon as one gull moved away, another moved in to stab and bite soft young flesh. One of the children, the larger and the elder of the two, was screaming and flailing her arms around, trying to use her bucket and spade in a desperate defence. The small child seemed to be in shock and stood there with her arms down by her side, not making any effort to resist the attack. Two women, perhaps the mothers of the children, were also screaming as loudly as they could while they watched the children being attacked without seeming to go to their assistance.

As Rork took to the air, adults closest to the incident ran to offer help. Most of the gulls turned towards the adults and took the attack to them. Two remaining gulls continued their attack on the children unhindered.

Rork took all this in as he strove desperately towards them. He entered the fray directly above the youngest child and struck her attacker a sharp blow with his feet. The attacker was Torg! Torg turned towards Rork, his eyes blazing madly, blood dripping from his beak. Rork lunged forward, using all his size and weight to drive Torg away from the child. He was faster and more powerful and there was only ever going to be one outcome. After a few hammering blows from Rork, Torg gave up the unequal struggle and flew off, leaving Rork in a quandary. Should he pursue Torg to finish him once and for all, or should he fight off the other birds? It only took him a millisecond to decide on the latter course of action and he turned into the mobbing birds, screaming loudly. To his horror, he saw the Admiral in the centre of the furore being attacked by three or four smaller but much younger gulls simultaneously. Rork could see that the Admiral was struggling for speed and agility but turned to the more urgent task of ridding the younger child of her attacker. This was a gull unknown to Rork, but one that was a lot better and braver at fighting than Torg. Rork could see they were both about the same size as each other and probably of a similar age. Rork crashed into his opponent, sending him spinning towards the sea. The strange gull recovered himself and turned to face Rork, screeching obscenities as he did so. The two of them clashed, thrusted and parried, with each of them striking telling blows to the other's body. Rork saw blood on his opponent's neck and had the satisfaction of feeling his feet rasp across his face, but this only served to spur his adversary on and Rork realised that he had a tough fight on his hands.

Suddenly, as if it at a signal not heard by Rork, the unknown bird broke off the fight, vowing to continue it to the death – Rork's death – at a later time. He turned and joined his colleagues in battle against the adult humans. As he did so, Rork saw Ensil dropping feet first to join the fray, quickly followed by the other birds detailed from the ground attack squadron. The remainder of the bitter skirmish became just a blur as Rork waded in to help his colleagues. After an exhausting few moments that seemed to last much longer, Rork and his smaller allies seemed to be getting the better of Torg and his renegades, when all at once four deafeningly loud bangs shook the air. All the birds scattered in different directions, with Rork making instinctively for the harbour light where he thought he might link up with the Admiral again.

The Admiral had indeed regained his former position and was standing there somewhat dishevelled, panting heavily. As Rork approached, to his utmost horror, two further shots rang out, striking the Admiral heavily and propelling him to the base of the harbour wall. Instinctively Rork dropped to his side, spreading his wings wide to shield for the Admiral from further harm. A lot of shouting was going on, but Rork was unaware of most of it.

He did hear a woman scream out loudly, "Don't shoot, you stupid fools. You've shot the wrong ones. Leave them alone."

The Admiral was still conscious and looked at Rork with a heartbreaking appeal in his eyes.

"I gave as good as I got, Rork," he managed to croak.

"You certainly did, Admiral," agreed Rork. "Please don't try to say anything."

The Admiral gazed back at Rork and shook his head very

slightly. Rork could see the light was fading from the Admiral's eyes and had never felt more helpless. He sensed another bird landing next to him and felt the bird dipping under his outspread wing.

"Let me see if I can help, Rork." Dew bustled in and took charge to Rork's great relief. After just a few brief moments of listening to the Admiral's breathing and examining a wound on the side of his head that pulsed blood, Dew turned to Rork and sadly shook her head too. Rork gulped and moved closer to the Admiral.

"You'll be fine," rasped the Admiral, then his great body shuddered and he passed away.

Rork turned to Dew who was visibly shaking and upset, despite her years of experience tending to sickly and elderly gulls. "I tried to find you, Rork. I tried to tell you that Torg was hiding in the rocks near the hospital." Dew was crying. "Are you alright?"

It was Felicity Dawson who had screamed so urgently at the men with guns. Anne and Steve found her sobbing uncontrollably by the carcass that once had been the Admiral.

"Do you see what those idiots have done?" she managed to get out between great convulsions of her tiny body. "They shot at this grand old bird when all he was really trying to do was stop the other birds attacking those children."

Anne put a comforting arm around Felicity's shoulders. "We know Felicity, we saw it happen. It was dreadful."

"They were so brave. Just this big old feller and that younger one, against all those others." Felicity gestured towards Rork. "He seems to have taken the old one's place, doesn't he?"

"It certainly looks like that," agreed Steve. "Look, the poor bird is trembling. Do you think he is injured too?" Rork was indeed trembling but trying desperately not to show it.

"No. I don't think so. It was the other one they were trying to get." Felicity turned towards the two men with shotguns who were still looking around at what they had done. Other members of the little protest group were berating them and were joined in the task by Felicity. "How stupid have you two been? Do you realise what a terrible mistake you have made?"

One of the men made an effort at defending himself. "They were attacking two little girls. Did you expect us to stand by and let them do it?"

"Oh, you absolute morons! The birds on the harbour light that you shot at were not with the ones that attacked the girls. They were peaceful gulls!" Felicity was beside herself with anger. The two men decided that silence was the discreet option and moved away from the small crowd at the harbour entrance. Felicity returned to Anne and Steve. "How many more birds did they kill, did you see?"

Her question was answered by the spotty-faced youth from Greenpeace. "At least another three birds were shot dead in their first salvo." He paused for a moment as the noise from an approaching ambulance siren drowned his words. "Their bodies are on the beach. I think another two were injured. One is just floating in the sea over there." He pointed about 50 metres out to sea where a gull sat motionless in the water with one wing outstretched.

The group of them watched as the team of paramedics efficiently went to the aid of the two small girls who were lying huddled under beach blankets, too shocked even to cry. One of the mothers was crouched down with them, while the other one was being comforted by a man, presumably her partner. Quite a large crowd stood around them, watching what was going on and discussing what had happened. Another siren announced the arrival of a local police car from which a police constable and his sergeant disgorged themselves to join the paramedics.

"How dreadful it must have been for those poor children." Felicity turned her attention to those on the beach.

"They really have some awful injuries," agreed Steve. "I just hope that it doesn't scar them for life, physically or mentally. Luckily, I don't think the birds attacked their eyes."

"There really are two groups of gulls, aren't there?" Anne had been thinking deeply about what she had seen. "The vast majority of the gulls were part of the fly-past and seemed to be trying to get their message across to us. A sort of protest demonstration, I suppose you could call it. It seemed to be working in their favour – the fly-past got a popular response."

Felicity eagerly interrupted her. "You're right, and the other much smaller group of gulls are the troublemakers, the vicious ones. They're the ones who deliberately seemed to set out to provoke us and to get us to react."

"And it worked," said Steve soberly. "Those idiots with their guns just saw all of those birds in that melee as the same and shot them without distinction."

"If they've been watching all day and have failed to spot the difference, think how the ordinary members of the public are going to view it," Anne lamented. "Steve, I've got to write the final article for the front page, please!" she beseeched him. "I've got to explain the difference or there will be a massacre."

"I was just going to say exactly the same thing," agreed Steve. "Get on it straight away if you can. Make it around fifteen hundred words maximum. I'll phone the office and tell them to prepare for it. Then I'll go and see Mickey to see what he's got from earlier that we can put with it."

Chapter 17 – The Last Hurrah

Rork's decision to take the Admiral's place on the harbour light was instinctive. Rork did not even think about it, but if he had he would have reasoned that it was what the Admiral would have wanted, and to do anything else would have shown weakness to the men that were trying to kill them. When Dew flew off to see if she could help the injured gull in the water, Rork started to shake uncontrollably and couldn't have flown properly had he tried. He was pleased that Dew was not there to see him in such a state, let alone Ardyl, Krom and the others.

Rork desperately tried to pull himself together. He needed to think about the implications of Torg's latest raid and the impact it would have on the major operation he had planned which was destined to take place in a short while. He watched while the noisy vehicles came to collect the injured girls and was pleased to see the smallest one talking animatedly to her mother. The small convoy departed just as noisily. He was also pleased and relieved to see the men with guns walk away but this swiftly turned to concern when they turned into a building adjacent to the harbour. He had just regained a degree of self-control when Dew alighted back beside him to be followed a few moments later by Ensil.

"There was nothing I could do go for that poor bird in the water," Dew explained. "He had lost too much blood. The little thing was crying for his mother. He was so young, which is probably why Torg managed to get him to join his side. The poor creature passed out while I was with him and without any means of supporting his head, he drowned. There was nothing I could do to prevent it." Dew looked appealingly at Rork.

"I am sure he was comforted by your presence, Dew. I know that the Admiral was. It seems you were right all along and that our efforts to stop the men's killing spree have only lead to further disaster." Rork's head was bowed as he said this. Neither of the other two birds had seen him like this before. Ensil loyally and desperately tried to revive his leader's spirits.

"D...d...don't think like that Rork! E...e...even if we had n...n...not embarked upon the dirty bomb campaign, just as many of us would have been k...k...killed at the land fill site anyway."

Dew's wing reached out to touch Rork lightly on his shoulder, causing Rork to take in a great gulp of air. "It was a very good plan, really Rork. It is not your fault that the violence shown by Torg and his followers created so many problems for it. Torg doesn't care whether he lives or dies and I don't think he cares whether anyone else does either." Dew's words were meant to comfort Rork and they found their mark. They gave back some of the reassurance Rork so desperately needed.

"I felt that we were winning the hearts and minds of the people, little by little. Some of them were even cheering when we flew over. But what will they think now Torg has attacked those two defenceless little ones? What on earth can he have been thinking about?" Rork was glad he had two of his closest friends to confide in. They acted as the sounding board he so desperately needed. The gap left by the deaths of Barff and the Admiral was a huge one to fill in so many ways.

"Can't you see, Rork? Torg's whole aim in making that attack was to cause as much shock and horror as he could. Unfortunately for us, he seems to have succeeded." The way Dew looked up at Rork as she said this made Rork wish for a moment that he could go far away with her and leave all his problems behind. Ensil interrupted his brief reverie.

"L… L… L… Look. Here they come!"

At the far end of the beach, above the cliffs that started there, the three friends could see the approach of a mass of birds, skimming over the short grass of the headland that led down from Potton Hill. The beach had returned to relative normality, especially at that end. Not one of the holidaymakers relaxing there had any inkling of what was about to occur. Which was exactly as Rork and the others had planned. The combined forces of Ardyl and Krom's heavy brigades swept overhead without warning and in a matter of seconds they had achieved coverage of virtually all the beach. At a command unseen and unheard from the harbour wall, the huge throng of birds released their cargo of dirty bombs as one. The effect was instantaneous. Hardly a family or a group were unaffected by the bombs in some way or other. Rork and the others could see hits on bare skin, clothing and all the beach paraphernalia that is so essential to the British holidaymaker.

A roar of anger swirled along the beach and as the last of the birds swept out to sea, some of the men even threw stones at them, although all of their missiles fell pitifully short. Even the television crews had been caught unawares and only managed to catch the chaos that ensued on the beach and literally the tail ends of the birds as they retreated out to sea.

By now, holidaymakers and the watchers were experienced in the manner of the gulls that attacked in formation and they knew to expect an imminent second attack. Binoculars and television cameras and eyes were therefore trained on the large formation as it manoeuvred out at sea. The keen-eyed spotted other birds joining the formation and it wasn't long before they warned that the birds had turned for another approach. This time there was no attempt at a surprise attack. The birds took almost the same line and method of approach as they had when making the fly-past earlier in the day, although they were

156

not flying nearly as high. Because the beach had been the target area a few moments before, the holidaymakers there collectively prepared themselves for another onslaught. Men with guns ran quickly down to the beach, calling the swimmers in to the shore as they stationed themselves at the water's edge in readiness. The mass of gulls approached steadily, without seeming to hurry at all, and it was obvious that they wanted the attention of everybody for maximum effect.

On the beach, people raised beach umbrellas or stood under those that were already raised. Those without beach umbrellas made temporary shelters from beach mats or windbreaks while continuing to clean themselves of the earlier mess. Those on the harbour wall watched these preparations and some wry comments were exchanged where the two groups were nearest each other, to everyone's great amusement. Then the cry went up that the formation was in fact heading towards the harbour and would miss the beach altogether. The boot was now well and truly on the other foot and it was the turn of those on the beach to laugh as they watched the spectators on the harbour wall hurriedly seeking some form of shelter. There soon came the realisation that portable shelter around the harbour was in short supply, so doorways, shop canopies and beneath balconies became popular points of refuge. The men with guns ran back up the steps of the harbour wall and took positions along it. Felicity Dawson, the spotty-faced young man from Greenpeace and some other braver protesters took up the same positions in order to deter the shooters.

Rork noted that the smaller birds from the ground attack squadron were stationed on the right-hand end of each line of their larger brethren, exactly as he had planned. Ardyl and Krom were in their customary leading positions. He turned to Ensil anxiously. "Gosh, I do hope this works."

"Surely you cannot let them do this, Rork?" Dew was

puzzled and could only see disaster ahead. "They are going to be annihilated by the men with guns."

Ensil laughed, unnerving her still further. "W… We do hope not, Dew!"

Rork turned to her. "We are trying to show that we are an intelligent species and that we don't want violence in any form. We have to show them that this is just our way of protest. Watch!"

As he spoke, the two huge flocks of birds closed with the harbour entrance. So profound was the silence, the beat of the gulls' wings could be clearly heard. No words or calls were uttered. Suddenly, as if by Rork's command, each bird in Ardyl's squadron made an individual abrupt turn to the right, each rank then being led by a smaller bird. In an instant the whole square had changed direction by 90 degrees and was heading for the beach! Guffaws of laughter from those reprieved on the harbour wall, and shouts of anger from those in imminent danger on the beach, grew in equal proportions as each side realised it had been tricked. When Krom and his squadron reached the same point above the harbour entrance, it too abruptly changed direction toward the beach using the same method. When the two formations had achieved overhead coverage of most of the beach, the second cargo of dirty bombs was released.

The operation had gone exactly to plan and Rork was just about to say as much to his colleagues when a barrage of shots rang out. Rork was aghast to see at least ten birds from the rear of Krom's formation fall to the sand, mortally wounded. Other birds started to straggle, showing that they too had received wounds. Dew prepared to take off to see if she could help those on the beach but Rork stopped her.

"It will be too dangerous for you down there. You can't do anything for them. Follow us to the quarry and help any wounded that manage to get back there. See if any of your colleagues can help. Ensil, follow me. Quickly!"

"Those of you who have followed our news stories this week will have been intrigued by our top story from Barlmouth regarding the strange behaviour of the local gull population. The gulls have been mounting ever-increasing attacks on the residents and the large number of visitors to this idyllic harbour town. Now, stories of gulls attacking humans have been around for a long time, but it is the scale and manner of these attacks that makes them so remarkable. The gulls are mounting raids in large formations, and instead of striking their target with their beaks or their feet, they are dropping what can only be described as dirty bombs with great accuracy. Mark my words, these are not random attacks but appear to be carried out with great purpose. You may recall the effect one such attack had on a local fishing party. Well, as they say, you ain't seen nothing yet. We have just captured on camera the most remarkable behaviour of any group of birds seen anywhere in the world.

"We came here this morning prepared to film sea gulls because we heard that more attacks were taking place, but when we arrived, there was not a gull to be seen. Suddenly, out to sea, our cameras picked up a huge flock of seagulls coming towards us in formation.

"Okay, we'll stop there and run film of the fly-past this morning."

Caitlin Johnson put the microphone down by her side and turned to her camera crew. "I need to know what shots we are going to include so I can do a voice-over for it. Let's move on to this afternoon's first attack." When the cameraman signalled that he was filming, Caitlin continued. "This afternoon, the gulls' behaviour took a sinister turn and became very violent. Some of you may find the following piece of film quite unpleasant and possibly upsetting to watch. Any young children and those of a nervous disposition, please look away now. My camera crew and I were standing on the harbour wall, waiting for the gulls' next move, when we were surprised by a loud disturbance not fifty metres away from us where another group of gulls was attacking two young girls. The girls were little more than toddlers. They had been paddling and playing at the water's edge of Barlmouth's sandy beach without a care in the world when suddenly this vicious attack took place. Both girls are now in hospital being treated for severe cuts and bruising to the face and body and are both said to be in a state of shock." Caitlin paused for effect. "Well, wouldn't you be?" She looked at her camera crew and gave a slight nod.

"Now, we going to run the film again but this time we will slow it down a little. I want you to look closely at what is happening. You will see the two little girls being attacked by maybe a dozen gulls, when suddenly a second group of gulls flies down to defend them. A fight then ensues between the two groups of gulls that is broken up by marksmen, with shotguns firing up into the melee of birds. Several gulls were killed by the four shots fired and the remaining gulls were scattered. Further shots were fired to kill a large gull that had only made it as far as the harbour wall. We have not shown close footage of the kills being made, as we are aware of the time this is broadcast and the number of children who will be watching." Caitlin lowered her microphone and fidgeted with her collar.

"Okay Ben, let's get the local RSPB man in at this point and see if we can get his comments." Caitlin turned to seek out Nick Pacey. She turned to the camera once more and waited for her colleague's signal to begin.

"I'm joined by Nick Pacey, who is a local businessman here in Barlmouth, also a long-time of member of the RSPB and a man who has studied the local bird population for many years. Nick, have you ever seen gulls behaving like this before?"

Nick squinted at the camera and gave a nervous cough. "I have seen a single gull make the odd attack on a human being in the past, normally because it is defending a fledgling which has fallen to the ground, or just because it bears some sort of grudge. But no, I have never seen a collective of them behaving in this way."

"It may be my imagination Nick, but the attacks seemed to fall into two categories. On the one hand, the birds are attacking in formation, and although they are dropping their dirty bombs on people and their possessions, they are not making any physical contact. There seems to be another smaller group of gulls who are simply vicious and who are striking out at people indiscriminately." Caitlin smiled encouragingly at Nick and pointed the microphone at him.

"I don't think it is your imagination. I would agree that there seems to be two sorts of gulls," said Nick cautiously, "but I don't think there's anything indiscriminate about either group of them. The larger group of gulls are using formation flying to show us what they're capable of and are dropping their faeces to reinforce this in an almost humorous way. A smaller group of gulls are much nastier. They are choosing their moments to attack isolated individuals. This morning they picked on a milkman, later a paperboy, and this afternoon, as you've just seen, they attacked two young girls who were incapable of defending themselves and who were separated from their parents by just twenty yards. I think in both cases, the gulls knew exactly what they were doing and this is what makes their behaviour so unique."

"That's it, thanks Nick. That was brilliant. I now want to bring in the lady from the art gallery, Felicity what's her name." Caitlin deftly moved across to Felicity Dawson and asked to be reminded of her surname. "I'm joined now by Felicity Dawson, who runs an art gallery in Barlmouth which by coincidence is called The Cry of the Gulls. Felicity, I think you have a theory as to why the gulls are behaving like this?" Again Caitlin smiled encouragingly at Felicity Dawson, who needed neither encouragement nor her confidence boosting in order for her to speak to the camera.

"It's not at my theory, you understand," she began. "My friend, Anne Rigby is a local reporter for the *Western Morning News* and she has discovered that local businessmen have been carrying out a secret cull of our gulls for the last few months, resulting in hundreds of deaths. This is despite the gulls being a protected species. In order not to leave any trace of what they were doing, the men have been shooting the gulls at our local land fill site where the bodies of the gulls could easily be covered up. We think the gulls are using this unique combination of formation flying and dropping their dirty bombs as a form of protest to get us to stop this happening. Every time they have flown like this, they have continued to fly in formation all the way to the landfill site and the only purpose of that can be to reinforce their message."

Caitlin withdrew the microphone from Felicity. "But it's not just gulls flying in formation and dirty bombing, is it? There have been some vicious attacks on people, as we have just witnessed."

"Yes, I agree there does seem to be a small and nasty group of gulls who are demonstrating their anger in a more direct way. But I'm sure the vast majority of the gulls are peaceful in their intent. These so-called marksmen that have been bought in by the council are not caring that there is a difference between the two sorts of gulls and are firing willy-nilly at them. If they are allowed to carry on, they will kill hundreds of innocent birds, so they have to be stopped!"

At this point, the spotty-faced youth from Greenpeace called out, "And we're here to damned well stop them. If they carry on murdering the gulls, we are going to attack the council offices in return."

Felicity did not let this interruption distract her. "You have to excuse my excitable young friend, but he feels very strongly about this. We believe that once the authorised and the unauthorised killing (of the gulls) stops, then the attacks by the gulls will stop too." Felicity's 'young friend' then started to chant "stop the cull, stop the cull. stop the cull." The cry was taken up by most of the other protesters standing nearby.

Caitlin Johnson reached down and took a large bottle of spring water from a capacious cream leather bag. She thanked Felicity for the interview as she unscrewed the top from the bottle and took a large, unladylike slurp from its contents. She turned to Ken Broadwell who had been standing nervously by, dreading this moment.

"Come on Ken, let get it over with. It's your turn now. You know what I'm going to say and what I'm going to ask you. I just want to find out if you can justify what is going on here."

Ken Broadwell adjusted his tie and pulled his jacket down at the back, squaring his shoulders as he did so. Images of his father suddenly flooded into his mind as he carried out these routine procedures that his father had drummed into him in his youth. He almost looked down to check if his shoes were clean; the thought amused him and put him in a better humour. "Ask away Caitlin, but don't make me look stupid. I wasn't born yesterday."

"I'm here with the Mayor of Barlmouth, Councillor Ken Broadwell, who has been watching the events very closely all day. Mr Mayor, I understand you authorised the posting of men with shotguns around your small town with instructions to kill the gulls. Isn't that a bit extreme?" Caitlin smiled as she said this but all Ken Broadwell could see was the teeth of a crocodile.

"With instruction to kill *aggressive* gulls, Caitlin. You missed out an important little word. There have been three vicious and unprovoked attacks on our townspeople already today, each of which has resulted in serious injury, necessitating hospital attention. You filmed the last attack in which two young girls suffered a horrifying ordeal inflicted by a mob of unbelievably nasty birds. Even if the poor kids recover from their physical scars, I think they will suffer the mental consequences for years. We can't allow that sort of rabid behaviour to continue unchecked." Ken Broadwell mentally notched up the score as one each.

"Is it true, Mayor Broadwell, that there has been at an unauthorised cull of seabirds carried out on council property for months on end? We understand from the RSPB that gulls are a protected species under the law." Caitlin wanted to prick the bubble of this big blustering man's pomposity.

"I have heard these allegations, Caitlin, and we are looking into them. As you say, any such cull will have been unauthorised by the council and we are aware that gulls are a protected species. However, a licence exists for us to cull them if there is a danger to public health and safety. You can see from your footage that the danger clearly does exist." Ken Broadwell thought he was edging in front at this stage.

"This afternoon we witnessed an extraordinary mass attack by the gulls, that shows, at the very least, that they have highly developed organisational skills. Some would say they show great intelligence, maybe even a sense of humour. What is your take on this?" Caitlin lowered the microphone at this point. "What we will do here, Ken, is to run the footage of the last attack when the birds fooled everyone as to their intentions." She raised the microphone towards Ken's chin once more.

Ken anticipated what was coming. "I don't subscribe to this view that gulls have human type emotions of fear, anger or humour even. But let us suppose they did. What sort of joke is it to defecate on someone to demonstrate a point of view? For how much longer would Barlmouth have its tourist industry if our seagulls were allowed to continue with that sort of behaviour?"

"There are many who would disagree with that point -of -view Councillor Broadwell. Surely an intelligent demonstration, even if it comes in the form it did, should be met by an intelligent response?" He is just so unbearably smug, thought Caitlin.

"What sort of *immediate* response would you suggest,

Caitlin?" Ken Broadwell was unable to cope with the rhetorical question and realised his own reply was weak.

"Surely it is wrong to use weaponry just to blast away at a flock of birds without considering a more peaceful and less harmful course of action? We can see here an incredibly clever manoeuvre by the birds being met by the brute force of your gunmen. Is that a proportional response?" Caitlin sensed she had Ken Broadwell on the back foot.

"If it prevents just one more child being injured by these mad birds, then yes it is. It certainly is." Ken Broadwell settled for a draw.

Chapter 18 – Armageddon

Rork and Ensil followed the last of the two formations as it made its way up over the Downs towards the landfill site. Progress was slow, presumably because Ardyl and Krom had deliberately ordered the birds to fly slowly to allow the injured stragglers to keep up. So slow, indeed, that they were soon joined by Dew and two of her colleagues from Turan's cave.

"Turan has urged us to lead the injured gulls back to her cave, Rork. I can see at least eight that are in some form of trouble. May I get them to turn around and follow us back into the cave? It will give them the best chance of recovery." As Dew spoke, the last of the gulls, which had been struggling desperately to keep up for some time, dropped suddenly out of the sky and plummeted towards the ground. The pathetic bird hit the sun – baked earth with such force that they all knew it had no chance of surviving the impact.

"Of course you may." Rork agreed to the suggestion readily. "Please go to them straight away. If any of them are in any doubt, please say it was a direct order from me and that I will visit them as soon as I have the opportunity. Please be sure to thank Turan for me."

Dew and her colleagues went about their task immediately and each took two or three of the injured gulls under their control. Dew's small group was the last to leave the formation and Rork was pleased to see Dew raise her wing in an encouraging gesture as she turned back towards the cliffs. It seemed her anger at him had been forgotten, or that the reason for it had been forgiven.

Rork flew on in silence for a while, and Ensil misinterpreted this as sadness. "Being in Turan's c...cave will give them the best ch...chance, won't it Rork?"

"Of course it will, Ensil." Rork agreed. "It will also be better for the others not to see their injured colleagues when they reach the quarry. Morale will need to be high for what we are about to do." Rork was also pleased that Dew would not be there to learn about the final operation he was planning. He knew she would oppose it and he didn't want his resolve weakened, or to let anything affect the determination of the other gulls. He kept these thoughts to himself.

Rork had spoken so grimly that Ensil decided not to question him further. They flew a little faster now without the encumbrance of the injured birds but not a word was spoken until they reached the quarry, where Rork was pleased to see Ardyl and Krom lead the squadrons in to land, still neatly maintaining formation. The birds were given the instruction to eat their fill and relax for a while. Ardyl and Krom posted lookouts to patrol the sky above the quarry and then flew over to join Ensil and Rork. They ate together in a corner of the quarry, conscious that the eyes of the rest of the birds were upon them and that there was much expectation upon their shoulders.

Rork broke the news of the death of the Admiral to Ardyl and Krom, and when they had absorbed this sad blow he told them of the death of Barff and of the relationship between the two birds.

"Father and son. Phew, whoever would have believed it!" Ardyl was astounded by the revelation.

"When I think back to some of the wise things that Barff said to me, I can hear the Admiral's voice in some of his words." Krom spoke with great sadness and then he rose up to his full, considerable height. "Damn their eyes. Damn their eyes. The absolute swines! To kill two of the noblest birds this land has ever known Rork, you know we must avenge them."

Ardyl looked expectantly at Rork, Ensil stopped eating and looked up at Rork and Krom waited in silence for a reply to his statement. It was at that moment that Rork realised the Admiral was right. Rork *was* the natural successor as leader, and there was no one else for him to turn to. He had never felt so utterly alone or afraid in his life. The responsibility of what was to come was his and his alone and the prospect terrified him. The lives and future of all the birds in the roost depended on what he now had to say. He spoke quietly and simply to them, telling them of his last conversations with the Admiral, of the Admiral's preparedness for his own death, and finally of his wish for Rork to become leader of their colony.

Rork's three colleagues listened without interruption until this point. "You know he didn't make the choice alone, Rork. I was just one he consulted and I endorsed everything said about you. You have my utmost unflinching support for anything you ask us to do." Ardyl broke off, unable to speak further.

Krom clapped Rork on the back with one of his huge wings, desperate to cover Ardyl's embarrassment. "A lot of us have seen you as leader for some time now, Rork. As far as I'm concerned, this does not change a thing. Someone's got to do the serious stuff," he joked. "It might as well be you!"

Ensil felt compelled to speak. "E…e…ever since we were g…growing up together, I have felt you were d…d…destined for great things, Rork. I will be proud to follow you anywhere."

Rork thanked them for their kind words. "When you hear what I have to say, you may not feel as generous towards me." He outlined his plan to them. They listened in complete silence until he had finished. No one spoke for what seemed an eternity to Rork, so in the end he said, "Well?"

"Let's do it!" uttered Ardyl.

"Let's do it!" agreed Ensil, his eyes wide open and bright.

"Let's do it!" roared Krom, causing hundreds of pairs of eyes to swivel towards them.

"Right. Get the squadrons into some loose form of order. I need to speak to them." Rork turned busily away, concerned they would catch a glimpse of the raw emotion he was feeling.

A few moments later, Krom reported that the squadrons were ready for his address. Rork leapt upon the upturned remains of an old pushchair and turned to face the gulls. There were no comic remarks, no barracking, in fact no conversation at all. The mood was serious.

"There is no easy way for me to break this news to you all. The Admiral is dead." There was silence for the briefest of moments, then a collective gasp came from the crowd of birds. "The Admiral should have been allowed to die a dignified death of old age. He deserved that; he has served us so well. Instead, he was blasted from his favourite position on the harbour light, barely an hour ago, by men with guns who could not distinguish between one good gull and another rotten one. As if that was not bad enough, earlier today his son was killed too." Another round of gasps of amazement swirled around the birds, forcing Rork to pause again. "You may not know that Barff was his son. I didn't myself until earlier, but now that I do, it all makes sense. Many of you know more of the kind works of Barff than I do. Many of you benefited from them. You have known him longer. I only knew him a matter of days, but already I feel a great sense of loss. You must feel this loss more than I.

"We have *all* suffered grievous losses at the hands of these murderous gunmen; close relatives, loved ones and friends. At least ten members of Krom's Cronies were killed or seriously injured as they left the scene of the last raid." A deep swell of anger emanated from the assembled birds. "We have tried to communicate peacefully with the people of this town, but to no avail. Torg and his followers have tried other ways, attacking the young and defenceless in a wild and irresponsible manner. That was the coward's way, and it has only served to anger those that previously may have been drawn to our side." Murmurs of assent followed this remark.

"Consider this. Are ordinary people our enemy? Are ordinary gulls a threat to them?" This caused the gulls to look at each other and the muttering became so much that Rork was forced to pause for a while as they considered his questions.

"Perhaps all of us have been attacking the wrong targets. It is the men with guns who are our enemy. It is them who are killing us and it is them who we should be attacking!" This met with a universal roar of approval.

"They are out in the open now. We are going to take the fight to them, just them. We are going to attack those holding guns – only them and no one else. Do you understand?" This time the roar was deafening, and Rork had to wait quite a while before it subsided. When it did, Rork spoke quietly but clearly.

"I want all of you to listen carefully to our plan. You big guys in the two heavy brigades will fly in formation out to sea and back towards the harbour again. You will mount a dirty bomb attack in the disciplined and brave way you have learnt to do. We will select an opportune target in the harbour itself. You will fly in low enough that the men will open fire on you, but high enough to make it difficult for them to aim and to do damage." Rork paused to allow the birds to mutter to each other while this sank in.

"Make no mistake, there will be casualties." He paused again. "Once the men with guns are out in the open space of the harbour like they were earlier today, I will lead the ground attack squadron over the town at rooftop level, to avoid being seen until the last possible moment. As we are coming in from the opposite direction to you, all eyes should be upon you, allowing us to get our first strike in with total surprise. We will not be dropping dirty bombs on the gunmen. We will be hitting them – as hard as we possibly can." Another roar of approval swept through the assembled birds.

"We will continue to strike until the men lay down their weapons. Although there are not many gunmen, we can expect a lot of casualties." Rork paused once more to let the gulls absorb the implication. "Make no mistake, it will be a pitched battle. You heavies will be held in reserve. Ardyl and Krom may bring you in to inflict further damage, but remember, it is only the gunmen we wish to hurt." Rork looked across at Ardyl, Krom and Ensil.

"You have not had an opportunity to think of me as your leader. You have not been given the opportunity to discuss it amongst yourselves. It is your right to choose another." Rork paused, but if he was expecting a challenge, none came. No one moved. No one spoke.

"What I am asking of you is extremely dangerous and will result in the death of many of you. I know some of you will not agree with this plan. There is no shame in that. Let me be absolutely clear, there is no shame in flying away now. No one will think badly of you."

Still no one moved. Still no one spoke. For a few seconds, there was utter silence. Then feet started to shuffle and the shuffle grew into a stamp. Without any spoken command, the gulls formed into lines, each bird a perfect distance apart. Each line matched perfectly with the next. Ardyl, Krom and Ensil marched to the head of their respective squadrons and each turned to face Rork. The stamping of webbed feet continued.

From the back of the throng a cry went up, "Ror-ork! Ror-ork! Ror-ork!" It quickly spread along the ranks of gulls and swelled to deafening proportions.

Rork turned, stretched out his wings and led his gulls into the air. A television camera crew arrived at the top of the road leading into the quarry just in time to film them taking off.

Anne returned to the harbour to find Steve sitting alone on the harbour wall, watching the group of protesters arguing amongst themselves. He was holding his mobile phone to his ear but broke off his conversation shortly after she arrived.

"They like your article as much as I do, Anne. It's in print as we speak. We've gone to press slightly early today."

Anne looked tired and drawn. "Which of Mickey's photographs did you use?" she asked.

"We used three in total on the front page, and they are going to use a lot more inside. The first was a shot of the last formation just before it changed direction and the second shot essentially showed the same picture seconds later, after the manoeuvre. That was designed to fit in very well with your piece on the intelligence shown by the gulls. Mickey had been very clever in using the harbour light with the gull on it as a reference point. The third shot was a close-up of the gulls clearly fighting each other over the top of the little girls. Its composition is so good it should win an award in its own right. We had to show the behaviour of the fanatical gulls in order to highlight the distinction you made between them."

"I think it's all going to be very much 'yesterday's news' as you describe it." Anne said disconsolately. "I've just spoken to Nick Pacey. Mayor Broadwell and his cronies have drafted in another dozen or so guns for this evening. They are planning to go to the roosts and slaughter as many birds as they can find." She flopped down on the wall and sat dejectedly with her hands on her lap.

"I know," replied Steve sympathetically. "I saw some of them arrive a few minutes ago. I think they are farming friends of Councillor Clifton from the way they were greeted by him." Steve bent his head closer to Anne's. "I have done something which I think may help cheer you up."

"I'm sorry, I didn't mean to sound miserable," said Anne, looking up with just the ghost of a smile. "What have you done?"

"I've arranged for a hundred or so copies of tomorrow's paper to be brought over here tonight. They should be with us in about an hour."

"That's brilliant!" cried Anne delightedly. "We can give

172

them out to the men with guns and the people around the harbour to get them to stop this stupid killing spree. They won't dare carry it out as they will be too frightened of public reaction when people learn the truth." Anne touched Steve gratefully on the shoulder and ran over to Felicity Dawson and her colleagues to tell them. Steve watched the animation in her face as she spoke. He thought how lucky he was that this oddest of stories had brought them together.

"They are going to help us distribute them," Anne almost skipped back to Steve as she said this. To his infinite surprise, she kissed him on the cheek. "I'd like to buy you a drink, Mr Gooch!"

Steve acquiesced happily and they walked around the harbour towards the Victory Hotel together. Suddenly, Anne's mobile phone rang from somewhere in the depths of her handbag. She paused, looked up at Steve apologetically and answered it. The colour drained from her face as she listened intently.

"It's too late," she said desperately, switching off the phone. Her legs felt rubbery and she urgently wanted to sit down. "That was Lenny Hewitt. All the gulls have just taken off from the quarry and they are heading this way!"

Bryan and Erica Jordan were sitting on the 'opportune target' in the harbour that the birds were to select for their final raid, but both were blissfully unaware of their imminent demise. They were sitting in the sunshine on the first super yacht ever to enter Barlmouth harbour, and were quietly toasting themselves with small glasses of champagne before the imminent arrival of their guests.

Morning Glory was called a super yacht because she was over one hundred feet long, was over twenty-five feet in the beam and had a massive draft of 12 ft to the bottom of her huge bulb keel. She was brand new and every inch of her stainless steel bright work shone immaculately, from the tip of her pulpit to the pair of boarding ladders on her stern. Not a mark blemished her navy-blue fibreglass hull, which shone with reflected light from the gently moving waters of the harbour. Her teak laid decks had been scrubbed yet again, even though they were already perfectly clean. She was dressed over all with signal flags reaching to the very top of her gleaming white carbon-fibre mast, and other bunting festooned her boom. A navy-blue awning was erected over the perfectly proportioned teak gangplank, and although it was still broad daylight, deck lights shone ready for the evening's celebrations.

All around Bryan and Erica, people busied themselves preparing for the party. Paddy Cassidy, the yacht's professional skipper, oversaw the loading of yet more cases of finest pink champagne to be laid in boxes of ice brought over from the fish dock. Three employees from the yacht manufacturers' yard in Southampton were below working on some minor electrical problems that Paddy and Bryan had discovered during the yacht's maiden voyage to Barlmouth. Waiters from the Waterside restaurant bustled up and down the gangplank bringing serving plates groaning with seafood and salads, canapés and confections. Tables outside the Waterside restaurant had been moved aside and a small wooden dance floor had been laid close to *Morning Glory*. A string quartet tuned their instruments in one corner as crowds of tourists stood on the harbour wall, mouths agape.

Bryan and Erica had come a long way since growing up together in Barlmouth through the fifties and sixties. This was to be their coming home, their moment of triumph, the cementing of all their achievements in the eyes of their contemporaries. Ostensibly the reason for their visit was to allow Bryan's mother to officially name *Morning Glory*. As she was an elderly and wheelchair-bound lady, if she couldn't get to the yacht, then the yacht must come to her. As it was, in order to show off *Morning Glory*, Paddy Cassidy had to spend

174

many hours studying the tidal patterns needed to allow the super yacht to enter and leave the harbour. Other boat-owners had been gently bribed with invitations or simply money to move their own vessels away from the quayside in front of the restaurant. Luigi had agreed to close the Waterside to any further bookings that day, in return for a fee that could only be imagined. The source of Bryan and Erica's wealth had always been the subject of much local speculation, with people surmising that it came from a variety of enterprises ranging from drug dealing and smuggling to a huge lottery win. In fact, it came by the dint of hard work running a factory in West London, combined with the good fortune to sell not only the business to a multinational conglomerate, but also the land it occupied to property developers. *Morning Glory* was Bryan and Erica's treat to reward themselves for the hard years they had put in, and she was due to take them slowly around the world in their retirement.

Promptly at 6 o'clock, the quartet started to play something appropriately nautical by Benjamin Britten, and the guests started to arrive. The dress code was nominally smart casual but as this was one of the most anticipated events of the calendar for the great and good of Barlmouth, no expense had been spared, particularly by the ladies. Although most of the men dressed relatively conventionally in navy blazers, yacht club tie, white slacks and deck shoes, most of their wives had gone to town – some of them literally! Those that hadn't ventured into Plymouth or Exeter had delighted the owners of the Blue Water Chandlery, giving them its best month's sales figures to date. The guest list read like a Barlmouth's *Who's Who* and among those honoured were the mayor, Councillor Clifton, Alex Dunwoody, Derek Marsden and of course their wives and partners. It was just as the guest of honour was being slickly whisked up the gangplank, still in her electric wheelchair, that the first sighting of the approaching gulls was announced.

Bryan Jordan and Paddy Cassidy had heeded earlier warnings and were prepared. They quickly organised the unfurling of the yacht's bimini to cover the area where the food was laid, and for another navy blue awning to be spread over the broadest part of the foredeck so that most of the guests could be accommodated under its shelter. Barry Clifton and Derek Marsden quietly made their excuses and left *Morning Glory* to find their guns.

Ardyl led his squadron towards the harbour entrance at an unhurried pace to be sure they were seen by those on shore. He tried to exude an impression of calm and to instil confidence in each of his followers but inside his heart was pounding and his breathing was faster than normal. He hoped that he had chosen the correct height and mentally prayed for the safety of the birds that followed him in grim silence. His keen eyes spotted the glittering hull of the *Morning Glory* as she lay stern to the quay by the Waterside restaurant. He took in the activity that surrounded her and immediately decided that she was to be the target. He flew back to the leaders of his squadron to inform them and sent one of them back to Krom to let him know it too. He rose slightly to look back at Krom and saw him shout delightedly and nod. By the time they reached the entrance to the harbour, Ardyl could see gunmen spread along the harbour wall between his flock and the large yacht. Undaunted, he pressed home his attack.

Before the gulls could even release their cargo of dirty bombs, the men blasted away with their shotguns. This pleased Ardyl because if he had not drawn their fire, the early stage of his mission would have been deemed a failure. Unfortunately he learned they were in range of the guns by the many pieces of shot that zinged past him. As he reached directly over the yacht's mast, he released his cargo and wheeled to his left over the water of the harbour. Had he looked towards the town end of the harbour, he would have seen Rork leading the ground attack birds into the fray.

Rork led his gulls low over the roofs of the town and, as they wheeled around the church steeple and crossed Market Square, he swooped even lower to lead them into Fore Street, barely above head height of the people shopping there. They entered the harbour, skimming so low that they caused pedestrians to duck or jump out of the way, but the gulls were going too fast to hear their curses. Rork could see the gunmen pointing their guns skyward towards Ardyl's flock and could see smoke billowing from the guns as they fired. His eyes took in the huge yacht and the throng of people massed on its decks and smiled grimly to himself in agreement with Ardyl's choice of target. He could see dirty bombs raining down on the decks but unfortunately he could also see three of Ardyl's flock crashing down too.

Rork selected a tall and heavily built man as his victim, thinking that he looked vaguely familiar. Had this man shot at him in the quarry? He flew into him beak-first with all the speed that he could muster. He hit him behind the head with such a stunning blow that for a moment Rork thought he had broken his own neck. He heard the man cry out with pain and had the satisfaction of seeing him topple into the harbour. He soared upwards and turned to watch the mayhem below. He was closely followed by Ensil, who was wearing a delighted look on his face. Rork surmised he had struck at his target equally well. The surprise element was totally with the gulls and in the midst of the furore he had the satisfaction of seeing Faz and Jez making strikes too. From a safe height, he watched Krom's birds deliver their payload with such great accuracy that the navy blue of the boat's awnings changed to speckled grey and purple, interspersed with the odd patch of navy blue. To his chagrin, he could also see a large number of birds down, either in the water or by the harbour wall.

With most of his own birds safely gathered around him, Rork rallied them for a second attack. Ensil protested vehemently. "Rork, you know we agreed that you would take no further part in the attacks after the first one. It will be too dangerous. You are our leader now and we cannot run the risk of you being injured. You must go to the harbour light and watch from there, as we agreed."

Rork considered this for all of two seconds. "I appreciate what you are saying, Ensil, but I need to go down for just one more time. Follow me!" Without waiting for further argument, Rork led the way back over the rooftops. Ensil looked at the others helplessly, shrugged his shoulders and followed. They regrouped a few streets away and Rork turned to them.

"They will be expecting us to come in from the same direction, so to make it difficult for them we will come in low along the beach and swing up over the harbour wall to make an attack. And yes, I did mean swing *up* over the wall. I want you to fly at zero feet at the edge of the sand."

Again, before any discussion or argument could take place, Rork swept down towards the beach. Ensil could see that Rork's blood was up and felt elated and fearful as he followed his leader down. Rork led by example and skimmed the water's edge just a few inches from its surface. Once or twice they had to swerve to avoid a paddler but it was all part of the exhilarating joyride that Rork took them on. Soaring up over the harbour wall and veering to the right, Rork saw the group of gunmen looking about them at a largely empty sky. Without hesitation, he repeated his headlong charge and struck one of the men squarely in the chest. The man grunted loudly but didn't go down. Rork soared upward and turned to see how the others fared. He saw most of his birds hit targets; among them Faz and Jez successfully landed vicious blows. Suddenly he realised that Ensil wasn't with him and he panned wildly about to locate him. Almost at once he spotted an injured gull coming to ground at the end of the harbour wall near the harbour light, and he knew in the pit of his stomach that it was Ensil. He instructed his flock to hold their next attack, until the second raid of the heavy brigades distracted the gunmen, then he swooped down towards the harbour light.

He and Dew reached Ensil at the same moment. Rork was experienced in death by now, he had seen enough of it in the last few days, and he didn't need Dew to tell him that Ensil was mortally wounded. Rork dropped down by Ensil's side and nuzzled into his head. Rork knew that Ensil was in extreme pain and felt guilty about leading the last attack instead of him. Had Ensil had the extra few seconds' advantage of surprise instead, he may have come through unscathed. Ensil desperately tried to hold it together. "So f…f…f…effing futile!" he said, and died.

Rork did not look at Dew. He flew on top of the harbour light and looked over the battleground. Dew flew off towards the fighting without saying a word.

From his viewpoint, Rork could see that the battle was going badly for the gulls. Although many of the gunmen had dropped their weapons and were holding parts of their bodies in agony, still more held their guns to their shoulders in anticipation of further attacks. Rork had severely underestimated their numbers. The large yacht was covered in faeces and many of the guests' fine clothing were ruined forever. Defiantly, the quartet was still playing and waiters still moved among the guests, plying them with champagne and nibbles. Rork could see the bodies of at least 20 gulls lying around the harbour wall or in the water. As he watched, the large awning on the boat's foredeck sagged to one side with bird droppings dribbling from it. Sadly he watched the body of a dead gull roll off it and into the water.

Without any warning this time, the remnants of the two heavy brigades appeared overhead and it became obvious that they were aiming not at the yacht, but at the gunmen themselves. At the same moment, Rork's own gulls flew into the attack, coming in low from the town end of the harbour. The unmistakable figures of Faz and Jez made a strike and

Rork watched as they sped across the water of the harbour. All at once he saw Faz disappear, leaving just a cloud of feathers floating gently down onto the water. Jez turned in horror as he witnessed the death of his brother. Rork thought for one awful moment that he was going to turn to attack once more, but instead Jez wheeled around and flew high and far out to sea. Rork followed his progress as far as he could, but even his keen eyes lost track of Jez as he headed towards the horizon. Rork was pleased that he had flown away, reasoning that he was too young to fight and that he needed to find a new, safer home elsewhere.

On the harbour wall there was evidence of death and destruction everywhere. Bodies of gulls littered the pavement and the water. James Hawkes cleaned blood from his shotgun – his own blood! He thought his cheek had been broken by the impact of one of the gulls. Certainly some of his teeth had been dislodged and he was spitting blood every few moments. Derek Marsden sat on the ground, covered in blood and faeces. A woman was tying a form of bandage around his head and blood was already seeping through the cloth. Barry Clifton was still standing uninjured but soaked to the skin, and was ruing the loss of his favourite shotgun. A television crew filmed the debacle while its excited reporter tried desperately to describe all that was happening.

Felicity Dawson was comforting one of her friends. Other protesters were screaming obscenities at the men with guns and some of them were screaming back in return. One of the men put down his gun and punched the spotty-faced youth in the face. The string quartet played on.

"Here they come again! Guns at the ready."

The scene became something that Anne Rigby later described as one from her worst visions of hell. Caitlin Johnson described the gunmen as 'being filled with a terrible bloodlust' and likened the action of the gulls to Japan's kamikaze pilots of the Second World War. The battle continued to rage for a further twenty minutes, with both sides suffering a lot of casualties. The difference between the two sides was that the gulls' casualties were more often than not fatal. Adult holidaymakers came up from the beach and most of them sided with the protesters to such an extent that the gunmen were literally jostled and barged even as they took aim. Mickey Featherstone took hundreds of photographs. Some were savage, most were sad, a few were tinged with humour. All of them were poignant.

Dew came back to the harbour light, infused with so much anger and emotion she could barely speak. "For pity's sake Rork, how much more do you want to see? Call it off! Please!"

Rork had been considering doing just that as Dew flew down and berated him. He saw a huge body of people surrounding the men with guns and knew they were on the side of the gulls. But he could also see that the gulls could not suffer this rate of attrition for much longer. The volume of screaming and gunfire rose to epic proportions when, surprisingly, it began to quieten quite quickly. Faces on the harbour wall turned and looked out to sea. People on the beach stood up and called out to their children, pointing seaward in alarm. A dark black cloud was gathering in size on the horizon and as Rork and Dew watched, they could see it change shape and form. As it grew, they could see it was rapidly approaching Barlmouth. The remaining gulls flew out of harm's way to watch, and many of them flew down to the harbour wall to join Rork and watch from there.

The ominous cloud swirled and grew ever bigger. As it neared the little seaside town, a cry went up from the watching gulls. With their keen eyesight, they could make out that the cloud was made up of the largest flock of birds any of them had ever seen. Soon, people armed with binoculars realised the composition of the cloud too and the word quickly spread amongst the crowd. The protesters cheered wildly.

As the massive flock approached the harbour, the gulls

could see it was being led by the diminutive figure of Jez, flanked by Wingco and Loddo. So vast was the number of birds that the air was filled with the sound of their beating wings. Not just gulls were in the flock. All sorts of seabirds were there, from cormorants and shags to oystercatchers and terns. All the members of the huge crow family were represented, as well as songbirds such as the thrush and the blackbird. Ducks and geese abounded. The sky filled and darkened with their shapes silhouetted against the deepening blue of the evening sky. At a given command, unheard by those below, the birds dispersed and landed wherever they could find space around the harbour. They filled rooftops and gutters, railings and walls, cabin tops and decks. So many water birds floated on the water of the harbour among the dead and injured gulls; there was hardly a space between them. Three pairs of swans settled nearest the men with guns and looked up at them expectantly. The remainder of the gulls from Rork's colony flew on to the wall close to him. Space was made for Wingco and Jez, and the huge forms of Krom and Ardyl. Dew stood beside him.

All avian eyes and human eyes were turned towards the men with guns. The string quartet stopped playing and a deep and profound silence replaced the hellish cacophony of a few moments earlier.

As they looked about them at the thousands upon thousands of birds gathered around, the men lowered their guns.

One of the men laid his gun down by his feet. One by one, the other gunmen followed his example, until all had done so.

A child started to clap with excitement. One by one the people followed *her* example and soon, all did so.

182